the Christmas Tree Keeper
-a novel-

the Christmas Tree Keeper

-a novel-

TAMARA PASSEY

Winter Street Press

Winter Street Press
winterstreetpress@gmail.com

Cover Design by Laura J. Miller 2014
www.anauthorsart.com

Library of Congress Control Number: 2014920142

ISBN-13: 978-0-9909840-6-1

1. Christmas–Fiction 2. Trees—Fiction 3. Miracles—Fiction

For Steve

PROLOGUE

Hans and Adeline Shafer, Germany, 1880

He watched her unpinned curly hair fly as if in protest. The wind howled a farewell through the trees as he reached for her shoulder.
"It is time."
She buried her face in her hands, dropped to her knees, and cried despairing tears. The wind subsided; a quiet stillness amplified her sobbing and the soft, breaking sound of her tender heart at leaving the only land she'd ever known.
He knelt beside her, watched her tears fall to the ground, and whispered gentle words of love. He cried too and cupped the tear-stained earth in his hands and put it in his leather pouch.
"Hush now. It will go with us to the new world."

CHAPTER 1

The Nor'easter brought the snow, but that didn't start it. The radio station began playing carols around the clock, but that didn't start it. Main Street wrapped the lampposts in candy-cane-striped garland, but even that wasn't enough. Not until the decorated tree stood in the front window with soft lights glowing around the angel's contented face did Christmas officially begin in the Donovan family. This year, Angela promised her daughter she could have the honor of choosing the tree.

"Is this the one?" Angela asked as she held her daughter's hand and stared at the four-foot pine tree.

Caroline leaned closer to it. She closed her eyes and took a deep breath. "Do you feel that?"

"Feel what?" Angela asked.

"The tree. She's beautiful," Caroline answered.

Angela bit her lip and glanced at her watch. "Does that mean you want this one?"

Caroline stepped back and spread her arms like she was measuring and gathering the tree's majesty. "Looks like two broken branches on the lower right," she declared with the certainty of a triage nurse. "Pretty, but I don't think so." She skipped ahead to the end of the row. Angela followed her daughter. Gravel and pine needles crunched under her feet and strings of white lights crisscrossed above her head. "I'll Be Home for Christmas" played from a speaker hanging on a light pole. Nostalgic words for most people, but unless she could come up with more rent money, they wouldn't have *any* home for Christmas.

She looked to her right and left. The line of trees formed a row like toy soldiers and offered no hint of how to get back to the parking lot.

"It's getting late, Caroline. They'll close soon."

It didn't matter that Angela had botched another job interview and had planned to stay home and cheer herself up with a little *Wuthering Heights*. No. There would be no English moors and brooding Heathcliff to take her mind off her bleak prospects. She'd promised her daughter they could bring home a tree. Angela's hope for the day to end better than it began was disappearing with every tree Caroline rejected.

Other customers strolled around them. Angela watched a couple huddled against the chill who looked more interested in each other than the trees. Her attention returned to her daughter, who had stopped walking.

"This is it. This is the one!" Caroline exclaimed.

"Are you sure?"

"Yes! I love it."

Angela could see the excitement on her daughter's face. This is what Caroline needed—something happy to focus on, to brighten the mood in their one-bedroom apartment. Maybe their holiday could begin on a hopeful note after all.

A rushing sound started in the tops of the taller trees. The branches on the shorter trees danced in the swirl of wind as a wiry old man approached them. He wore a round, red *Shafer Farms* pin on his heavy coat.

"Do you believe in miracles?" He looked Angela square in the eye and continued, "People say they do, but mostly, they just want to believe. There's a difference. Wanting to believe is a good place to start. The problem is, most people wouldn't know a miracle if they were standing right next to one."

"That's good to know," Angela said as she took a step back, forcing a smile.

"We have some Scotch pines right here. They hold their needles." He winked at Caroline. "And that's not all."

2

The man wasn't pushy, but Angela worried she couldn't afford what he might try to sell them. She nodded, hoping to get past his sales pitch. "Thanks, but we've found the right-sized tree for our cozy living room."

"Why, sure you did. These here are Shafer trees, and they're special," he said. "They're miracle trees."

Caroline's eyes widened at those words and she squeezed her mother's hand. The man seemed to zero in on her fascination, and before Angela could put a stop to it, he filled Caroline's head with precisely the kind of nonsense she had worked so many years to keep out.

In a deliberate whisper, he said, "I can't tell everyone in Massachusetts this, but I have a feeling about you. I think you might need a Christmas miracle."

Caroline nodded while Angela tried unsuccessfully to interrupt.

"What you need to do is put up one of these Shafer trees and believe. Then you'll have yourself a Christmas miracle," he explained.

Caroline didn't waste any time. "Well, my mom does need to pay the rent."

Angela blushed at the words and looked around to see if anyone else could hear them.

"Is that right?" he asked as his eyes narrowed. "You need some rent money?"

"Thank you for your help. It's late and we need to go," Angela said impatiently, more so than she had intended.

"But Mom, don't you owe like a thousand dollars?" Caroline blurted.

Angela shifted her body too late to prevent Caroline from being overheard by an older couple walking the tree lot with their grandchildren. She looked back at the alarm on the salesman's face and her pulse quickened with embarrassment.

"Where can we pay for this tree?" Angela asked, purposely ignoring the discussion of rent and miracles and money. She wasn't mad at her daughter. It wasn't Caroline's fault she had to understand the realities of life at an early age. But did she have to disclose their wretched circumstances to a total stranger? Even if he was an eccentric Christmas tree salesman?

The man moved slowly to the tree and removed part of the tag. "Take this over to my grandson in that farmhouse. I'll have the tree brought out after we give it a shake and wrap it up." He handed the tag to Angela, but smiled at Caroline.

Aside from her daughter's uncomfortable admission, Angela might have enjoyed the walk across the festive lot to the farmhouse. She might have relaxed and allowed herself to feel the excitement of the coming holiday. But Caroline persisted.

"Did you hear him, Mom? All we have to do is *believe*."

"Oh, Caroline, if it were really that easy."

"What's hard about believing?"

Angela found the cashier inside the warm farmhouse. The glowing fire and smell of hot chocolate did nothing to stop her irritation.

"Is that your grandfather out there?" she asked, nodding toward the large window with a view of the tree lot, still exasperated by her daughter's newfound hope.

"Do you mean Papa Shafer?" the young man asked. "He's not my grandfather, but we all call him Papa. He's the owner."

The owner. Of course.

"Is there a problem?"

"It's just that—never mind," Angela replied, pulling her wallet out of her purse.

"Well, someone paid for your tree," he said as another man appeared behind the counter.

"I couldn't help overhearing. Are you unhappy with something here?" He put his hand out to shake Angela's and introduced himself as Mark Shafer. Angela noticed his broad shoulders and square-set jaw. *Attractive. Not what I need right now.*

She juggled her purse and wallet and fumbled to return the gesture. His hand was warm and as their eyes met, she confirmed what he looked like at first glance. *Definitely attractive.*

"Oh," she answered after too long of a pause, "I didn't know my daughter was going to hear about your miracle trees. Christmas is kind of hard as a single mom without getting her hopes up, you know, for impossibilities." Her words lost emphasis as she saw the genuine concern on his face.

How am I supposed to complain to this good-looking man?

She handed the cashier her credit card. He didn't take it. She looked back and forth between the two of them.

"I can pay for it," she insisted. *I'm not trying to get a free tree*, she wanted to add emphatically.

"What I was saying," he said, exchanging a look with Mr. Shafer, "is that a man paid a hundred dollars for your tree. He said to give you whatever change was left. Here, this money is yours."

The cashier held out three twenty-dollar bills. Angela scanned the room and saw the other customer who had been listening to them on the lot walk out the door. His windbreaker had a logo with a number she didn't recognize.

"Maybe you'd like a larger tree?" the cashier asked.

Angela stared at the money in his hand.

"Or if you're done shopping, I can make sure your tree gets taken to your car," Mark offered.

She took the bills from the cashier, now in view of her eight-year-old daughter's all-seeing eyes. *I'll figure out something else for the rent. And the Christmas presents.* She handed the money back and said, "I'm sure someone else needs this more than we do."

Angela grabbed Caroline's hand and walked out with Mark. He asked them what Papa Shafer had said about the trees. Caroline was glad to repeat it, and since Angela was having trouble finding her tongue, as well as her truck, she let her daughter carry on about how nice it would be for them to have a Christmas miracle.

She found her pickup right where she'd parked it. Mark took the four-foot tree from the employee who brought it up from the lot and lifted it into the bed of the truck. He insisted on helping, although he wore a cashmere coat with a tie peeking out from underneath it, and his dress shoes reflected the parking lot light.

She listened as he explained.

"Sounds like you met Papa, my grandfather. He's seventy-seven this year and loves the trees, the holidays, and especially the children. His imagination gets away from him. He doesn't mean any harm—I'd say he has a lot of pride in these trees."

Caroline sighed and her shoulders dropped. Angela could tell she was deflated, but she reassured herself, *better she hears the truth now than later.*

Mark called to someone a few cars away. "Hey, Nat, I'll be there in a minute!"

Angela saw a tall brunette leaning against a black BMW.

Great—we have an audience.

"So, what did you say your name was?" Mark asked.

Ignoring the question, she opened the door and motioned for Caroline. They jumped in the truck, and Angela pulled the door closed, overcome by a sick-to-her-stomach feeling at the thought of a woman waiting for this Mark Shafer, who—at the moment—was being detained by a frazzled, cranky customer. He did not need a name to associate with *that* scene.

Angela turned the key in the ignition. Her old, worn-out pickup truck sputtered.

No. Don't do this to me. Not now. "Start," she demanded.

"Is everything okay?" Mark called.

She twisted the key again. More sputtering.

He took a few steps toward her truck.

"Are we out of gas again?" Caroline asked from the passenger seat.

"No. That's not it," Angela answered, noticing the puzzled look on Mark's face.

She rolled down her window and forced a smile. "We're fine."

One more twist of the key and the truck started. She drove out of the parking lot, beyond the white fence, and onto the narrow, tree-lined road—the same road where, a few hours earlier on their way to the farm, they had planned how they would decorate the tree, drink some hot chocolate, and maybe even listen to some Christmas music. That was before they met Papa Shafer, before he told Caroline about miracle trees. Angela slowed as they reached the turn-off. She didn't look back.

"Do we get to put up the tree tonight?" Caroline asked wide-awake as ever.

"Let's put it up tomorrow when we're feeling better," Angela said.

"What do you mean? I'm not sick."

"A good night's sleep might do us both some good."

"I'm not going to forget what Papa Shafer said, if that's what you mean." Caroline declared.

"Let's call him Mr. Shafer—he's not our papa. How about we put the tree in the stand now and we'll decorate it later? We need a good rest."

"Mr. Shafer is the man *you* like," Caroline said.

"What are you talking about?" Was she that obvious?

"You were staring at him. Until you jumped in the truck, like when I used to run away from Brian Mahoney and you said I had a crush on him."

So much for subtle.

6

"Look, I just met him. Besides, well-dressed *and* handsome never works out for me."

"Papa Shafer is the one who said we can have a miracle," Caroline said.

"We didn't have to pay for the tree—let's call that our miracle. See? We're good."

"Getting a free tree was not it," Caroline said. "A nice man was probably spreading some Christmas cheer. Papa Shafer said we have to put *up* our tree and believe. That's how we'll have a miracle."

Angela didn't respond.

Doesn't she have enough disappointment in her life?

"You don't believe in miracles, do you, Mom?"

Angela heard the question and watched the road twist in front of her. It was dark as she rounded the corner. The stoplight changed from yellow to red. She sighed. What could she tell her daughter? She had believed in miracles once.

Angela gripped the steering wheel and held back every pessimistic thought. She looked at Caroline, staring at the holiday-lit houses and twirling a strand of hair. She pulled through the intersection, took a deep breath, and answered, "I believe miracles *can* happen."

"I knew it. I knew you believed." Caroline's face lit up and Angela's heart sank. That wasn't the impression she was trying to give. As if finding a job and paying the rent weren't enough pressure—now they needed their very own Christmas miracle.

CHAPTER 2

During its opening weekend, Shafer Tree Farm bustled with the energy of a family reunion. Loyal customers came to celebrate the start of the season. Mark watched their eager faces, the children a year older and a few couples with their first baby. Some came for Donna's crafts and hugs. Others came to be first on the lot to have their choice of tree. This was the weekend they prepared all year for, watched the weather forecasts, and hoped for mild temperatures and clear skies—or, if there was snow, at least passable roads. Maybe if Mark had a family of his own, he wouldn't feel like a visitor at his own farm.

He watched the old pickup truck roll out of the parking lot, curious about the woman driving it. She had a pretty face or a familiar one—or both. He reviewed what he'd told her about Papa and the trees. She left so fast. *Why didn't she tell me her name?*

He pushed his hands deeper into his coat pockets and walked toward the exit of the parking lot. As the truck disappeared beyond the thicket of trees, his focus turned to a small sapling shooting up outside the fence, not far from the edge of the asphalt.

Mark crouched down and brushed away some snow, exposing the ground. He slipped off his glove and felt around the base, the handle, of the miniature tree. He counted the branches and used his hand to estimate the height.

You're a gutsy tree but you'll get run over growing here by the road. I'll have to find you a new home.

He stood up and brushed off his hands. A picture of the fully grown tree outside his bedroom window formed in his mind. It was anyone's guess what his father had intended to do with that part of the ground he had cleared years ago. This new little tree would be a welcome addition to the view of the back of the craft barn. He looked at the tree once more and made a mental note to extend the fence to shelter it until he could move it in the spring. The wind picked up and he turned to face it. He saw Natalie waiting for him.

Oh, no—what time is it?

"Can we go? I'm freezing," she said as he approached her.

"I've got to go back inside to help close and check on Papa. Come with me."

Natalie looked steely eyed at the farmhouse. "How long will that take?"

"Not long, I hope. I have good news," Mark said.

"Well, what is it?"

"I'll tell you over dinner."

Once inside, Mark greeted Donna and Brett. The ever-cheerful Donna had stepped in when Mark's mother died to lend a helping hand. Twenty years later, she worked at the farm year round. "Where else would I go? All my favorite people are right here." she'd often say.

"Craft barn is closed," Donna reported. "You two look like you're up to something," she said as she glanced at Natalie.

Brett replied before Mark did. "Can't you tell, Donna? Look at him. I'd say they're headed someplace—"

"Expensive," Donna said, shaking her head.

"I was about to say boring," Brett teased. "But I bet you're right. Expensive, too."

"Just a little dinner," Mark said. "I was going to help with that register, but I think I'll check on Papa instead." He shot back.

"At least tell me what to do with this money," Bret asked. "This is the sixty dollars that woman wouldn't take."

"Put it in the hospital fund," Mark answered.

Natalie dropped into the wingback chair by the dark fireplace. She took out her phone, crossed her legs, and began swinging her foot.

"I'll talk to Papa and then we can go." Mark assured her he'd be quick. He found Papa in the back office staring out the window, as still as a Douglas fir.

"Hey, Papa, are you watching the trees grow?" Mark offered lightly.

"I suppose," he murmured.

"Customers are gone. It's late. I was hoping to lock up so I could—"

"Go already. Don't keep Natalie waiting. I'll lock up with Donna."

"Papa, why don't we all leave? You need some rest."

"I'll get my rest. You go. Let me have my peace. That's all I'm asking for on a day like today."

Mark bristled. The developer had called and offered again to buy the tree farm. Papa wouldn't even consider it. "Not in my lifetime or yours," he'd said. "We sell our trees, not our land."

"How about you come to a late dinner with us?" Mark asked tentatively.

"Of course not," he said. "Leave me be. The land is quiet tonight. The wind is blowing in from the north. The trees know there's a change coming."

"Papa."

"The trees know it, Mark. I don't yet. But there's something."

Mark kept his eyes from rolling. The trees *this* and the land *that*. He couldn't reason with Papa anymore. When he talked about the trees that way, Mark wished his parents were still alive. Maybe they'd understand him better, or maybe his dad would be able to explain the trees to him in a way that was at least rational. But that wasn't possible. He changed the subject.

"Did we get the name of the generous guy who paid for that woman's tree?" Mark asked.

"I don't show my face at the register, remember? You want me on the lot with the trees, and even that makes you nervous."

"Papa, it's not that. It's the stories. You have to be careful what you say to the customers. Like tonight—that woman wasn't happy about the story you told her daughter."

"I tell one story, and it's the truth."

"I know you think the trees are special, and to our family, they are." Mark inadvertently began the tired debate.

Papa turned and hit the desk with his fist, startling Mark.

"Are they? Are they special to you, my over-dressed grandson? Do you care about these trees and what they've done for our family? What they've done for the families in Sutton and all over New England for five generations? These trees saved my great-grandparents from starvation so you could be here today." Papa grabbed the edge of the desk with his shaking hand. "Now they bring joy to everyone who sees one or buys one. And you plan to sell them to some butcher, to someone who will make woodchips out of them faster than that little BMW of yours can get you to Boston. Go on." Papa's voice lowered with unusual fatigue. "Get outta here."

Mark backed up to the door and staggered out, stunned. Natalie stopped pacing by the fireplace when she saw him. Mark could tell by her wide eyes that she had heard Papa's outburst.

"You okay?" She buttoned her coat.

"Did anyone else hear him?"

Natalie shrugged her shoulders. "I don't know. Let's just go."

Mark couldn't dismiss it that easily. He scanned the room to see who remained. Donna focused on the counter and didn't look up. What did she hear? Did Papa tell her about the developer's call? Was she as angry as Papa, or just unhappy that he was dating Natalie?

Donna loved everyone—or *almost* everyone. Papa took care of the trees, and Donna loved the customers. He didn't have to ask her opinion of selling the farm—she'd offered it plenty of times. "For Papa's sake," she'd say, "keep the farm as long as you can." Couldn't she understand that Papa wasn't going to live forever? Shouldn't they sell before it got any harder to operate?

Instead of talking to Donna, he walked to the entryway, where he found Brett sweeping the floor.

"Will you make sure Papa gets to his cabin? Don't let him stay up front here alone. He can be stubborn."

"Like someone else I know," Brett replied.

"Yeah, I get it. Please make sure he gets settled—"

"Go have a good time. I'll take care of Papa."

"Thanks, Brett. See you in the morning."

On their way to the steak house in Millbury, Mark hit the brakes a little too hard for the red light. He felt Natalie reach for his free hand, but he kept his eyes fixed on the road.

"Are you thinking about Papa?"

"Yeah. The good news I had to share doesn't feel so good now."

"You can still tell me," Natalie said.

"Maybe when we get inside." Mark clenched his jaw and ended the discussion.

After their waiter led them to a table, she asked again.

"So, are you and Papa going to be okay?"

Mark sat against the high-back leather booth and noticed the expectation in her eyes. "He thinks that I think I'm above growing trees. And that's not it."

"You don't have to tell me. He doesn't understand your love for music. Or your business sense. There won't be a better time to sell the farm, will there?" she asked.

"That's just it. The developer called again today and offered more money." Mark scanned the nearby tables, cautious of familiar faces. Leaning in, he continued, "More money than we could get anywhere else."

Natalie smiled. "That's great news," she said matter-of-factly.

"Not to Papa. He won't budge. He won't even consider it."

Natalie looked at Mark with raised eyebrows. "That's why he has you. You'll help him see it's for the best, right?"

"Didn't you hear him? I'm his 'over-dressed grandson' who doesn't know what he's talking about. He won't listen to me."

"Then you have to make him listen. It's the only way you can buy your house, right?" she pressed. "How many houses in Sutton have a music studio in the basement? You can't sit back and watch that house go to someone else."

"I could find another way to buy the house," Mark said. "But it'd be hard if we don't sell the farm first. Besides, the music studio will sit empty if I'm working at the farm every day." He tensed. "Remember I told you when I was ten my parents died?"

Natalie looked up. "Yes, but what does that have to do with this?"

Mark continued, "I'd go to my room and listen to music as long and as loud as I could. That was my way of dealing. Papa had a different way—work. To this day, he lives to work that farm." He checked Natalie's face for a reaction. "What can I do now? I might have to wait until Christmas is over before I can try to change his mind."

They finished dinner and the table felt like it had grown while they ate, creating more distance between them. He needed closeness with Natalie, not more space. If he was ever going to propose, he needed more time than these late-night dinner dates allowed. How could he tell her that? And how could he ask her when there wasn't a chance she would agree to marry him unless he could get Papa to sell the farm?

Mark blamed himself for how much she disliked it. On their first few dates, she'd been so empathetic about the hard parts of farm work. She listened while he vented about weevil control, herbicide applications, and broken pruning equipment. Before long, she encouraged him to sell. "Your music can't wait forever," she'd said.

Mark paid for dinner, and as they left the restaurant, he played out "what-if" scenarios in his mind. If he could convince Papa to sell, if he could buy the house for a few thousand less, if he could buy it on his own. What was the use? Until Papa sold the farm, Mark would be at his side, keeping it going. And Natalie would be looking for someone else to date who didn't have tree sap under his fingernails.

"Who was the woman in that old truck?" Natalie asked.

Mark waited a minute before he answered, "Some customer. She was upset over Papa's storytelling. I had to smooth things over."

"Stories? What was it this time?" She smirked.

"Same story—Shafer miracle trees," he said lightly.

"Seriously, how long are you going to let him roam around out there, telling that to customers?"

Mark's back stiffened.

"I mean, I'm just saying, you love Papa, right? You don't want him embarrassing himself, do you?" Natalie's face appeared softer, but her words still cut.

"Papa loves the trees. He'll be working that farm until he dies," Mark said.

Natalie muttered something. "What was her name?"

"Who?" Mark asked.

"The unhappy woman with the little girl."

"I don't know. I mean, I didn't get her name."

I didn't, did I?

"She sure drove off fast enough—once her truck started, that is," Natalie said.

It was odd the way he felt, not knowing her name. What was it about her? He met so many customers each year. She was pretty, yes, but more than that. Annoyed with Papa, anxious to leave . . . *Am I always attracted to women who don't like tree farms?*

But there was something else. The way she'd given back that money with a mixture of pain and resolve in her eyes, determined. No self-pity.

"Mark?"

"What?" he answered, checking Natalie's face for clues for whatever he'd done wrong this time.

"You just passed my apartment."

He hit the brake and pulled a U-turn. He slid into the visitor parking space, hopped out, and opened Natalie's door for her. They walked to the door of her apartment, where he gave her a quick hug and kiss good night.

"Aren't you coming in?"

"I'm going to check on Papa," Mark said. "I don't like the way we left things earlier." He searched her face for some evidence of understanding. She stared back and shrugged.

"Then call me tomorrow," she said.

Mark headed home. His room off the main floor of the farmhouse had a window where he could see the backside of the craft barn, but if he looked far enough to the east, he could see if the light was still on in Papa's cabin.

And what if it was? Would he go talk to him, and what would he say?

Had anything changed? Could he convince Papa to accept the offer?

No. Not yet.

CHAPTER 3

None of Angela's warm-fuzzy memories of decorating their childhood tree included hefting said tree up a flight of stairs. The tree simply appeared in their house, installed, with branches like outstretched arms waiting to be adorned with jewelry. Glancing at the tree in the truck bed and then up to the porch light outside their second-story apartment, she reassured herself they could do this. Sure, carrying the tree was the kind of thing her ex-husband would have done, but it was just a tree, right?

Angela and Caroline managed the first flight of stairs. Then while Caroline ran and unlocked the door to their apartment, Angela stopped on the landing for a moment. On the next flight of stairs, the tree felt heavier with each step. Angela glanced up as Caroline opened the door and turned on the lights. Maybe looking away distracted her, or maybe the needles got under her skin as she adjusted her bare hands. Whatever the reason, her foot slipped and her hands lost their grip. Her shin collided with the stair and she collapsed in a momentary shock of pain.

The tree took off like a toboggan let loose on an ice-coated, snow-packed hill. It slid to the bottom of the stairs and might have flown right into the parking lot if not for the railing.

Caroline ran to the top of the stairs.

"What did you do to our miracle tree?" she yelled.

"You mean, what did that tree do to *me*?"

Angela stood and brushed pine needles off her coat. She and Caroline wrestled the tree out of the rail and into their apartment. As soon as the tree was up, Caroline assessed the damage—two broken branches and lots of loose needles.

"Mom, look at it. We have to decorate it tonight," she begged. "We have to."

"Okay, we can start," Angela answered despite her fatigue. *Caroline needs this*. She pulled the only box of Christmas decorations she owned from the back of her bedroom closet.

A string of lights, two packages of ornaments, and an heirloom nutcracker came out first. As Caroline busied herself with testing the lights and lining up the ornaments, Angela pulled out their stockings—a little matted from being used as a cushion for the ornaments. She fluffed and smoothed the faux fur. Her fingers traced the stitched letters of Caroline's name and the melancholy began. Oh, how the first few years of her married life were like those stitches—predictable and neat.

She left the half-empty box and joined Caroline. They strung the lights on the tree. The ornaments didn't take long to space out over the branches. Angela hung a gold piano ornament, pulled the string, and listened to the notes of "Silent Night." Her mother had given it to her to start what became their ornament tradition—all five years of it. There were no more ornament gifts after Angela married Todd.

"Where is the star?" Caroline looked into the box, bewildered.

"I don't think it's in there." Angela rummaged through the items on the sofa and uncovered the star. "I found it," she declared, turning to see a very quiet Caroline. Setting the star down, Angela moved over to her daughter.

"What's this?" She held up a smooth wooden box.

Angela offered a tender smile. "I forgot this was here. Here, let me show this to you." She gently held the familiar box and showed Caroline the hand-carved figures at rest in the black velvet interior. Angela's weariness slipped away.

With wide eyes, Caroline reached for the figure of Mary. "Where did this come from?"

"Did I ever tell you about Dona Florinda?" The name rolled off Angela's tongue with the appropriate Portuguese accent.

"Who?"

"My piano teacher," Angela said. "Her full name was longer—Maria Florinda Silva—but she let me call her Dona Florinda."

"And she gave you *this* for a present? Were you a good student?"

"Yes, but that's not the point. She came to my house for lessons when I was probably a few years older than you."

"Is that when you lived in Provident?" Caroline asked.

"Provi*dence*. Yes, Dona Florinda lived in Fall River, I think. One December after a lesson, she looked around and asked if we had a nativity set. We didn't. The next week, she brought me this gift." Angela stroked the open edge of the box and gazed over Caroline's head at nothing in particular. How young she felt sitting on the sofa as if she were ten years old again with her teacher beside her.

"Did you have to wait until Christmas to open it?"

"No. She insisted I put it out right away, or at least part of it. She told me her family set out a different piece of the nativity each day until Christmas. And on Christmas Day—"

"What? What did they do?"

"They set out the baby Jesus," Angela answered.

"Can we do that? Can we?" Caroline jumped off the sofa.

Angela laughed and pulled Caroline close for a hug. "Yes, we can. I don't remember the order, but she told me things about each piece. Like about Mary, the one you're holding, she said, 'Have a pure heart like this girl Mary, and you will receive the greatest blessings from heaven.'" Angela smiled at how the words came back to her in Florinda's rich, accented voice.

"What about Joseph?" Caroline asked.

Angela remembered exactly what Florinda had told her about Joseph, but was in no mood to repeat it to Caroline.

"It's getting late—very late. We can do this tomorrow."

She scooped up Mary and returned her to the box. Caroline protested with her sad face.

"What about the baby Jesus? What did she say about him?" she pleaded.

Angela lowered her eyes, "She told me to always remember that Jesus was born to make forgiveness possible for us and for others." She looked over at her daughter and noticed the thoughtful creases in her forehead.

"One more? Please, tell me about one more." Caroline pulled

the lamb from its place.

"You would pick that one."

Meu cordeirinho. My little lamb.

"That one was my favorite." Angela took it from Caroline's hand for a moment and then gave it back. "Florinda explained how important little lambs were to Jesus. Like a good shepherd, He knew their names and searched for the lost ones. I used to sneak that lamb to my room and take him places. I'd put him under my pillow, too. I thought I'd never get lost if I had him with me." Angela fought back unexpected tears, feeling lost for a long time now. "Come on, it's late. Time for bed."

As Caroline got ready for bed, Angela cleaned up the front room. She tied the star to the top of the tree. Before she pulled the plug on the tree lights, she stopped and looked at it.

Well, are you a miracle tree?

She found Caroline sitting on the twin mattress on the floor beside her larger bed, waiting.

"Where did you put the nativity set?" Caroline asked.

"I left it out. You can arrange it however you like—*tomorrow.*" Angela motioned toward the pillow.

Caroline plopped her head down.

"What kind of a miracle do you think we'll have?" she asked.

Angela shook her head, but before she could answer, Caroline continued. "We need more rent money, but I have another idea."

"Oh, you do, do you?" Angela braced herself for whatever new miracle Caroline had imagined.

"Wouldn't it be great if we spent Christmas with Grandma, and had, like, a big family celebration with food and presents and . . ."

Angela kept a straight face, but winced internally at the mention of her mother. Presents and dinner she could possibly pull off, but not her mother.

"Let's get some rest, Caroline." Angela turned away.

"So were you good at playing the piano?" Caroline asked, still with too much eager wakefulness in her voice.

"I practiced a lot."

"Why don't you play anymore?"

"I'm not sure if you've noticed, but our apartment is barely big enough for the two of us. Where would we fit a piano?" she said playfully. "Now good night." She turned off the light and heard one more timid question.

"Didn't my dad like music too?"

Angela squeezed her eyes shut.

Please, not more questions about Todd. Not tonight.

"Yes, he liked music, but you knew that."

"And didn't he like music more than us? Didn't he leave us to go sing in a band?"

Breathe. Yes, to sing in a band with a certain backup singer.

This wasn't a new conversation. Caroline had been asking variations of the same question for as many years as she had been old enough to understand that her father was gone and living in Florida. Postcards and once-a-year visits were the most she knew of him. Angela had given her answers. Caroline still asked why.

Will she always think he doesn't like her?

Angela sat down on the edge of the mattress.

"Look, sometimes people want a better life. And they *think* they know what will make them happy. They miss all the good people they have around them while they're chasing something else." She pulled the covers tight around her daughter and hoped the answer would be enough.

"Do you still like music, Mom? I mean, if you had a piano, would you play it?"

"Of course. Music is a beautiful part of life." *Some musicians, on the other hand, I could do without.*

"Do you think he misses us?"

"I have no idea what he thinks. But I'm not missing you. I'm right here." Angela smoothed Caroline's hair. "I'm glad we put up our tree tonight. And how much do I love you?"

"This much," Caroline stretched her arms out wide and Angela leaned in for a hug.

Angela didn't have any trouble waking her daughter on Saturday mornings. Caroline loved going to Mrs. Shaw's while Angela cleaned apartments. They bundled up for the walk to the building next to theirs. Angela reviewed the same list of manners for Caroline to observe.

"It's easy to be polite at Mrs. Shaw's place. She's never *cross*, like you, *Mum*." Caroline grinned.

"Don't mock her, for heaven's sake!"

"I'm not. I love the way she says things. Even when she's mad, it never sounds like it because of her voice," Caroline said.

"You mean her English accent."

"Yep, whatever it is. Don't worry. I'll be *have*."

"Good morning, girls," Mrs. Shaw said as she stood on her doorstep. "There's a chill today, isn't there?"

Angela smiled to herself. She loved listening to Mrs. Shaw too.

"We put up our tree last night. You have to see it!" Caroline squealed.

"Come on in now. How about you stay and have some breakfast, Angela?"

"Thank you, but I—"

Mrs. Shaw ushered her through the door, despite her protest. "You don't have to stay, but at least take a roll."

The apartment smelled of sweet citrus. "Are these orange rolls?" Angela asked. Unable to resist the warmth, she sat at Mrs. Shaw's kitchen table and ate with Caroline for a few minutes. She admired several of the handmade quilts displayed in Mrs. Shaw's living room, including a holiday-themed one she hadn't seen before.

"So you have your tree. I'm glad to hear it," Mrs. Shaw said as she moved about her kitchen.

"We decorated it and it's beautiful. Guess what else," Caroline said.

Angela narrowed her eyes at her daughter and shook her head. Maybe Mrs. Shaw picked up on the silent direction and took it as a cue to carry the conversation.

"My, it's so fun to decorate a tree. That reminds me of the year we had the ugliest tree in all of England. My sister demanded we carry it to our house through the back alley so no one would see it." Mrs. Shaw refilled the hot chocolate in Caroline's mug. "What a time we had trying to make that tree pretty. We used all of Mother's ribbon to reattach a broken branch and covered it with, oh, what was that called . . . angel hair." She laughed softly. "That's been a long time ago now."

"Do you miss living there?" Caroline asked as she licked her fingers.

"Sutton has some things that remind me of home—that's why I've stayed here for two decades. But everything in this country is so *big*, so wide. When I'm in England, I feel like I'm in a lovely cocoon," Mrs. Shaw said wistfully. "Every four or five years, I try to go back so I can feel like myself again. Of course, retired seamstresses don't have tons of money and now my daughter lives in Oregon, so my craft money takes me across *this* country instead."

"I'd better get going," Angela said. "Thank you for your help with Caroline today, and for that delicious roll. I should only be two hours today."

"So short? Only one apartment?" Mrs. Shaw asked.

Angela hesitated. "Well, Vivian told me she's hiring her granddaughter and Mrs. Kramer said she'll call me in the spring. Mr. Kramer started another round of treatment."

"Oh, you can't be getting by with only one apartment. Do you want me to talk to a few friends? It's no trouble, dear."

"No, thank you. We should be okay." Angela said quickly as she left. But it wasn't true. They weren't getting by, and they wouldn't be okay—unless she found more work.

Angela walked back home, grabbed her supplies, and headed out to Henry and Veronica's place. She hadn't advertised for cleaning work in the first place—she had offered to clean Mrs. Shaw's apartment in exchange for babysitting hours. Within a few months, she received calls from other residents who were friends of Mrs. Shaw's. They had heard what a fabulous job she did. Not likely—growing up, she hadn't cleaned more than her own room. But apparently Mrs. Shaw had a persuasive way about her.

She wondered each week if Veronica had cleaned before she arrived. She and her husband sat at their kitchen table and made small talk until Angela finished washing spotless windows and placed all of four plates in the dishwasher. This week they paid her a little extra. "For Caroline's Christmas," they explained.

Angela loaded the supplies in her truck and sat behind the wheel. Instead of eating lunch, she counted the day's wages. Holding her forehead, she strained to remember what she'd saved at home, willing the numbers to multiply to her advantage. No use. If her math was right, she was still three hundred dollars short for the rent due on the first of December, not to mention the other half of November's rent she still owed.

A partial payment will have to be enough.

Frustrated, Angela unloaded the cleaning supplies into the small utility closet adjacent to her apartment. She headed over to Mrs. Shaw's place to pick up Caroline. When she got to the bottom of the stairs, she saw the apartment manager walking with the maintenance man. She dug her hands into her pockets and tried to bury her chin into her coat collar, as if a bowed head might make her invisible. It didn't.

The manager sort of called her by name.

"Angie. Angie Donovan."

She hated that. Her ex-husband called her Angie.

She pivoted, pulled her chin up, and waited. He finished his conversation with the maintenance man and turned his attention to Angela, greeting her with a politician's smile.

"How are you, Angie? Say, I've been meaning to talk to you. You're harder to track down than a . . . a single mom. Wait, that's right. You *are* a single mom." He laughed.

Angela stared.

"So anyway, rent is due on the first," he continued. "No surprise there. But I need to tell you, the owners won't accept another partial payment. You can understand why, I'm sure." He rubbed his hands together. "You'll need to pay the full amount for December and what you owe for November, or I—I mean, they— will make me start proceedings." He scanned the empty courtyard with a pained look on his face as if he were the one facing eviction.

Don't they send letters for this kind of thing?

"Angie" echoed in her mind, triggering her sarcasm. *How awful that would be for you, poor Mr. Buckley. So much paperwork before the holiday.*

Only she didn't say it. Her faced remained motionless and she gave him a sideways glance. She wouldn't reveal her embarrassment or hostility.

"I'm working on it," she said.

He reached up to put an arm on her shoulder, and she quickly moved out of range. He lifted his hand without missing a beat and scratched the back of his head instead. "I've heard about the cleaning work you've drummed up."

"Actually, Mrs. Shaw helped me. I wasn't advertising."

"The office could use a deep cleaning, a going-over."

Angela's stomach turned. "Could we talk about it some other time? I've got to go. I'm late to pick up Caroline."

CHAPTER 4

Mark stood near the first line of trees on the back lot an hour before sunrise, waiting. A small wind rustled through the trees. It wasn't like Papa to be late. Even on mornings when Mark arrived early, Papa was there before him. Mark paced to generate some heat and glanced at his watch.

Something's wrong.

Papa lived in the two-bedroom cabin about a quarter of a mile east of the main farmhouse. It had been built by Papa's grandfather and the family had updated the wiring and plumbing to make it livable, although no one attempted to make it their home until Nana Shafer passed away. Papa packed his suitcase the night after she died and made the cabin his new home.

Walking up the path leading to the cabin's front door, Mark startled at a noise behind him.

"Looking for someone?" Papa asked.

"Geez, Papa, how'd you get there?"

"With my legs. How else?"

"I mean, I didn't see you."

"I'm moving slow this morning is all. Well, are we going to stand here and look at each other, or are we going to walk the lot?"

"I'll follow your lead," Mark said, relieved. They rounded the corner to the back lot and Mark slowed to Papa's pace. They exchanged a word here or there, but their silent walk among the trees had its own message. Mark didn't like to admit it, but he could tell Papa spent his time *sensing* the trees. Any conversation on his part would be an interruption to the important one Papa was already having.

Mark joined Papa in this tacit ritual a few weeks after his parents died, a month before his eleventh birthday. Mark hadn't expected to walk the lot until he was older—and with his father, not Papa. On those first walks, Mark felt oddly grown up, like the shoes he wore were a few sizes too big.

For all Papa's talk about the miracle trees, Mark never asked Papa what he did to understand the trees. He wasn't sure he wanted the answer. The quiet time suited him fine that way. The trees were as much a mystery to him now as they were when he was a grieving boy.

They walked off the back lot, through the front sales lot, and straightened the rows of pre-cut trees. They arrived at the farmhouse at the same time as Donna. She gave them a hearty wave and slipped in the front door. Papa stopped and held on to the wooden rail by the pathway to the farmhouse.

"The trees know there's a change coming," Papa said.

Mark didn't respond.

"I say there's a change coming. Do you know what it is?"

"I have no idea," Mark said.

"The trees are ready for a new keeper. Are you ready?"

"What do you mean?" *How do the trees know anything? How does Papa know what the trees know? Listen to me, now I'm not making any sense.*

"I'm asking if you're ready to run the farm. I'm not going to live forever. I've been waiting for you to get settled." Papa stood straighter, turned away from Mark, and held the rail with both hands. "When you met that Natalie, I waited for you to settle down some, but you've gotten more restless."

He thinks Natalie has done that?

Through a few breaks in the clouds, the first rays of morning sunlight spread out over the farm. Mark surveyed the farmhouse and trees while kicking some of the cold gravel with his feet.

Did he forget our argument, or is he ignoring it? What can I say? I'm ready to sell the farm, not run it.

"It looks like you need some time to think," Papa said.

24

Donna called from the back door, "Come on in before this breakfast gets cold."

A few hours later, Donna followed Mark as he breezed through to the back office. "You have two messages." She pointed to the paper by the phone. "This one is from some reporter from WCGB, Channel 6. He needs a comment from you. What's that about? And I don't know why I'm giving you this message from John Jackson, except for you to call him back and tell him there isn't a *for sale* sign in our yard."

"Thanks, Donna," Mark said. He avoided eye contact, and after she left, he closed the door. He called John Jackson first.

"John here."

Mark cleared his throat and introduced himself. Their conversation didn't last more than five minutes before Mark agreed to meet for lunch, no matter that it was almost twelve thirty.

He called the TV station and wondered what Papa had done to get their attention. The reporter explained he was working on a story about Sutton and their family-owned tree farm, and wanted a comment about the kind of trees they sold.

"Sure. We grow Fraser Fir and Douglas Pine."

"No, not the variety. I mean, what sets your trees apart from other trees?"

Mark wondered what Papa might have told him.

Was the reporter implying anything? Had he talked to Papa?

"We have pride in our Shafer trees, and we take good care of them. That's all." Mark ended the call and shook his head.

We take good care of our trees? What kind of a statement is that?

The conversation with the reporter might have bothered him all the way to the restaurant, but he had other things to worry about— namely why John Jackson asked to meet with him in person.

What does he think I can do?

He reviewed his conversation with Papa during their morning walk. Papa didn't say the farm needed a new owner—he said the trees needed a new keeper.

Can I do what Papa does? He and I are different. Dad knew what it meant to take care of the trees. Could I take ownership and then sell? Who am I kidding? There's no way to keep that from Papa.

Mark arrived at the restaurant and was seated at the table where

John Jackson was waiting.

"Glad you made it," John said after they shook hands.

"Do you live here in Sutton?" Mark asked. The town wasn't as small as it used to be—almost six thousand residents now. It was harder to spot the out-of-towners.

"I live in Quincy," John said.

"Do you usually do business around here?"

"I do business wherever my client needs land."

"And who is your client?" Mark asked.

"Let's not get ahead of ourselves. I figure it doesn't matter if I have a client who's willing to buy if someone isn't willing to sell. I get the impression from your grandfather that he plans to stay in the tree business forever."

"Pretty much," Mark said.

John continued, "Is that how you feel?"

"Not exactly."

"I could be wrong about this, but I'm not usually wrong. You want more than the farm life. Isn't that right?" John asked.

The waitress arrived with their order and set the plates down in front of them, giving Mark a chance to pause. John ignored his food.

"You could say that. The farm takes work all year round." Mark's throat went dry. He reached for his drink. He came to accept an offer, but now he felt defensive, and talking about the farm made it hard *not* to think about Papa and meeting John Jackson behind his back.

"So if you didn't have the farm to take all your time, what would you do?"

"I'd produce music."

"Music—*that* takes time. You can't do that when you're chopping down pine trees all day. Man that must be torture."

Mark winced, work on the farm was tough but he wouldn't call it torture.

"Here's what I can do for you," John began. Mark listened to his renewed offer, this time with an added incentive for Mark. "Sutton will be a perfect place for my client's auto dealership once they finish the construction of Route 146. Your grandfather doesn't see it that way, but you have to have your eye on the future. That would create how many jobs? Anyway, like I was saying, I'm offering you something for your help with your grandfather." John spelled out what he was willing to pay.

"You realize I don't own the farm," Mark said. "And convincing my grandfather to sell it isn't something I'm even sure I can do."

"I'm sure with this motivation, you can find a way," John said.

"And is the extra money legal?"

"I have a determined client, Mark. Don't you like to give your customers what they want?" John ate some bites of his lunch and waved down the waitress.

They stopped outside the door of the restaurant and John shook Mark's hand again. "I'm counting on you. I expect good news."

Mark walked unhurriedly to his BMW. What had he agreed to? As far as Mark was concerned, he didn't have to convince Papa to sell—he had to convince Papa he was ready to take over the farm. And since Papa had asked him that morning if he was ready, convincing him wouldn't be that hard, would it?

Not far from the restaurant, just off the turnpike, the Blackstone Valley shops had a small jewelry store. Mark checked his watch. *This shouldn't take long.*

"Can I help you?"

Mark stared at the rows of rings under the glass, unsure what to ask.

"I'm looking for an engagement ring."

The saleslady tipped her head. "Any particular kind?"

Mark sat down on the stool by the jewelry case.

"Sure. How about this one right here?"

"Does your girlfriend like the marquise shape?"

Marquise?

"Yeah." He had no idea. Mark watched the woman as she unlocked the case and put the ring in front of him.

"So have you looked at rings together?" she asked.

"No, not yet. I'm surprising her."

The saleslady explained the size and color of the diamond, and detailed the setting. Mark listened, but waited in vain to hear the price.

Natalie wore a teardrop necklace—maybe she liked that shape. Three rings later, Mark glanced at his watch and realized if he was gone from the farm too much longer, he'd have to explain himself. He looked at the princess cut one-and-a-half karat diamond ring in front of him.

"I'll take this one."

The saleslady, surprised by his declaration, stopped herself from putting the ring back and signaled her store manager. An older woman greeted him and asked about his soon-to-be fiancée while the other saleslady packaged the ring. She had a purchase agreement for him to sign. He handed over his credit card and looked one more time at his watch.

Driving home, he wondered how long it would take to have official ownership of the farm and how soon he could propose. He and Natalie were meeting for dinner after closing time, but he refused to propose at a restaurant. He pictured taking her to the house on Hickory Street with the studio—the place where they could start their life together.

I should buy the house first. As soon as I sell the farm.

Mark pulled into the crowded parking lot. He took the ring and placed it in his inside coat pocket, imagining the actual proposal. How had his father proposed to his mother? He wasn't sure why it mattered, but it bothered him that he couldn't ask them. But he could ask Donna—maybe she'd know.

Mark found her in the craft barn, talking to a woman buying several handmade wreaths.

"Hey, Donna, I need to talk to you."

"Right now?" she asked.

"When you're done, or when you have a minute." Mark ran his hand through his hair and waited. Donna finished the sale and smoothed her apron. She looked at the other customers, but didn't see any who were ready to buy.

"I have a few minutes. What's going on?"

"You were my mom's best friend, right? Can you tell me how my dad proposed to her? Did she ever tell you about that?" Mark's eagerness turned into sheepishness. A few minutes ago, this was urgent information, and now, maybe because of Donna's wide eyes and confusion, he wondered why he would even ask such a question.

"How your dad proposed? You're asking me now? Here?"

"If you have the time," Mark said.

Donna eyed a customer on the other side of the barn, pulled the stool from behind the cash register and pointed for Mark to sit down. She grabbed the broom and swept while she talked.

"I should've seen this coming. So your sister never told you?"

"Kate knows?"

"She asked me when she was fifteen. Girls are different that way. I figured she would've told you by now. Or you'd ask me—when you were ready." She emphasized the last word and looked at Mark. He shifted uncomfortably, like she was sizing him for a tuxedo.

"Are you and Natalie getting that close? Don't answer that. There's a reason I told you to sit down. Your parents weren't the most *traditional* couple."

Mark straightened up on the stool. "They weren't married?"

"Of course they were married. But you asked *how* your dad proposed. The short answer is that he didn't—at least, not with a ring or anything."

She stopped, held the broom, and stared at Mark before she continued. "They were good friends in high school, and your dad knew your mom liked him. About two months after graduation, he stopped by to visit your mom, and by the time they were done talking, they had decided to take off for Atlantic City."

"What?"

"Not what you were expecting, right? But remember honey, this was 1969."

"What do you mean? Dad didn't say, 'Will you marry me', but 'Hey, come with me to Atlantic City'?"

"I wasn't there for the conversation, but based on what your mom told me when they got back, I'm sure they talked about getting married before they left. That was the first thing they did when they got there. They found a justice of the peace and spent the next week at some music concert. Like I said, 1969—the summer of Woodstock."

"You're saying my mom and dad hung out at a music concert on their honeymoon?" Mark asked.

Donna set the broom down to ring up another customer. Mark stared at the snowman mitten keeper and the painted North Pole sign she bought.

"You okay?" Donna asked after the woman left.

"I'm fine." His voice wavered. He wasn't sure what kind of a proposal he was expecting, but this wasn't it. And hearing new information about his parents meant he had to adjust his image of them.

"If it helps, there's more to the story."

"Are you sure I need to hear it?"

"Your dad loved another girl in high school," Donna said.

"Okay, I've heard enough."

"No, wait. This will help." Donna continued, "They—your dad and his first girlfriend—planned to get married, but she went to visit family right after graduation, Maine or somewhere. When your dad went to ask about her after she'd been gone a month, he was told by her parents that she'd gotten engaged to another man. Your dad didn't handle it well. It was hard for him, and your mom—she understood. She was there for him."

"So Dad was on the rebound, and Mom went and married him in Atlantic City?" Mark stood up. "And you told my sister all this—what, fifteen years ago?"

Donna stopped rearranging the crafts nearest the cash register and moved closer to Mark. She put one hand up on his shoulder; she was a good foot shorter than he was.

"Not all love stories have the same beginning. They don't have to match some checklist for it to be real love. Your mom and dad loved each other. You know that, don't you?"

Mark nodded. "Yeah, I do."

"And they loved you and your sister, too. Your dad wouldn't have gone back into the house for your mom . . ." Donna stopped talking, and tears rimmed her eyes. Eighteen years didn't make a difference when it came to the pain of that night. Mark watched his dad run into the house when he realized his mom hadn't gotten out. That was the last time he saw him.

"Sorry, Donna. I didn't think we'd talk about the fire," Mark said.

"It's okay. I'm glad you asked—you needed to know. Believe it or not, there's more I should tell you—about your dad and the farm."

Mark held up his hands, indicating he'd heard all he could for one day.

"Good things, I promise," she said and sat down on the stool. "Wait—does this mean you and Natalie . . . are you proposing?"

Mark looked at his watch. "I'll catch up with you soon." He leaned over and hugged her. "Thanks, Donna. I don't know what I'd do without you."

Papa and I need to talk.

CHAPTER 5

Monday morning wasn't the greatest time for a job interview, but Angela didn't tell that to the school secretary who had called to arrange it—asking for a later interview time was a luxury she couldn't afford. The first of December was two days away, and even if she was hired immediately, she still needed more money for rent.

"Wow, Mom, why are you dressed up?" Caroline asked.

"I have another job interview today."

"Where's this one?"

Angela hesitated. "It's at your school."

"Really? Ooo, would you be my teacher's aide?"

"Uh, no, this opening is for help in the cafeteria." Angela took out two bowls from the cupboard.

"You mean you'd be a lunch lady?" Caroline said playfully.

"Only if I get the job, and that's a big if. Please don't say anything about it at school. It takes time if they decide to hire me. There's paperwork and a background check. And I'll still have to clean, too."

"So what are you going to do about the rent?" Caroline asked.

How could one simple question from her daughter be so painful? Did other girls her age think like adults and worry about the rent?

"I'm not sure, but I'll think of something. I always do," Angela said through her smile and clenched teeth.

"Why don't you call Grandma Elliott?" Caroline asked.

Angela set down the bowls on the counter. While she measured two parts oatmeal and one part water, she measured her words. "I haven't talked to your grandmother in a while."

"But maybe she could help us with rent. Isn't she rich?"

"In *one* way," Angela said.

"You mean there's more than one way you can be rich?"

"You can have a lot of money in the bank. You can also have a lot of love in your heart, and that way matters more than the money, I think." She checked Caroline's face for understanding.

"You once said she had so much money, she didn't know what to do with it all. She could give some to us until you get the lunch lady job."

"Do you remember everything I say? I don't have the job yet. Besides, you don't call someone and ask them for money." Angela's stomach turned.

Unless you're desperate. Am I that desperate?

Angela had moved to the innocent town of Sutton for two reasons. One, she loved it. Two, her mother didn't. They'd spoken twice in the four years since her father died. Her mother called a week after his death to make sure Angela saw the article in the *Providence Journal* about his contribution to the community. The other time, Angela called to give her their new address. All her mother had asked was, "Why do I need this?"

"Are you and Grandma fighting?" Caroline asked.

"I wouldn't call it fighting. We disagree about some things, but that has nothing to do with why I'm not calling her. We'll figure this out."

"Are you mad at her? Can she come for Christmas this year?"

"Why do you think I'm mad at her?" Angela answered the question with a question, ignoring her daughter's Christmas wish.

"Didn't she say your marriage to my dad wouldn't last?"

"Yes, but she said a lot of things."

"So, she was right," Caroline said.

She's eight. She's only eight. Take a deep breath.

"She also said nothing good would come of my marriage to your dad, but I have you. She wasn't right about that, was she?"

Angela regretted discrediting her mother to win the point, but she didn't regret making sure Caroline knew she was loved. "It's time to leave for school. Can you finish your oatmeal?"

In the rush out the door, Caroline stopped to admire the tree.

"The tree is even more beautiful than it was yesterday, don't you think? Maybe we'll get our miracle today."

"Now, hold on. It's just a tree," Angela said.

"Please *believe*, Mom. Let's see what happens."

She didn't argue this time. On the drive to school, her daughter's words echoed, "Just believe." Only the words were twisted, like Angela was six and school children were chanting them while she sat on the edge of the playground. Was it cruel, she wondered, to tell her daughter that miracles didn't happen? Or to let her believe one could happen any day?

She raced back home to get ready for her interview. She had twenty minutes. Her daughter's questions remained in her mind.

I'm not mad at my mother.

She's the one who disowned me. Who does that, disowns her daughter over who she marries? Why don't I call Grandma Elliott? She can call me. Any time.

Angela didn't try to understand her life. The day Todd proposed, she had expected to have everything she'd ever dreamed wrapped up with a bow, like the big satin one on the back of her lace-and-pearl wedding dress. Instead, her life unraveled, as if she had inadvertently pulled an errant thread, causing a slight snag at first, then an irreversible hole.

Despite the unraveling, there was one reason, one person, for whom she lived life moving forward—her daughter. Every time she looked into Caroline's pure and hopeful eyes, she saw a saving grace. Otherwise, she would still be retracing her steps, searching the far reaches of her closet for some stray thread.

She brushed her hair one more time and coated it with hair spray in honor of the job interview.

Maybe I'll call her just so I can tell Caroline I did.

She held the phone, staring through it.

And then what will I do? Do I want her money and what comes with it?

She dialed and the phone rang once, then twice.

I'm hanging up on three.

"Hello?"

Of course. She answers on two.

"Hi, Mom, this is Ang—"

"I know who it is. What's wrong? Is Caroline okay?"

"Why do you think something's wrong? Can't I call to say hi?"

Can't I hang up now and pretend this never happened?

"You said 'hi,' so what is it now?" her mother demanded.

This, Caroline, this is why I don't call your grandmother!

"Since you asked, no, Caroline isn't okay. She's kind of worried about the rent."

"You need rent money? Why didn't you say so? How much are you paying for that place? Are you still in Sutton?"

"I don't need all of it. $500 would help. I've been working, but not full-time. I have an interview today."

Why do I always start defending myself?

"I'm sure you need it by the first—how am I going to manage that? Do I have to drive all the way—?"

"No. Forget it. I only called for . . . Because I . . ."

"You aren't finishing your sentences. Do you need rent money or not?"

She does this to me every time. Doesn't she have a caring bone in her body?

"We need to stay here through December so Caroline can have a home for Christmas." *There—I said it.* "You don't have to drive here, there's a grace period. You can mail it or whatever's easiest."

"How would I even be able to find you?" her mother asked.

Doesn't she listen? "I said you can put it in the mail."

"Don't you live in one of those apartment compounds?"

"Complex, Mom. It's an apartment complex."

"Exactly and how would I find the one you live in?"

Am I really having this discussion?

"I'm in apartment 34, on the second floor of the Blackstone Apartments," Angela stated, as calm as possible.

"That's what I'm talking about. Why would they number a second-story apartment with a number like *34*?"

"I guess if you do drive here, you can leave a complaint at the office."

Angela finished the call, walked back into her bathroom, and splashed her face with cold water. She didn't even care that she'd already applied her makeup. She rushed to find her shoes and was stopped by a loud knock at the door.

This can't be an eviction. It's not the first of the month yet.

She opened the door to see a middle-aged man standing with an envelope in his hands. "Are you Angela Donovan?"

"Yes."

"Then this is for you. I'm supposed to tell you that *miracles happen.*" He turned and walked down the flight of stairs. Angela stared at the envelope, and by the time she looked up to ask questions, he was gone.

Miracles happen? She closed the door and locked it. She opened the envelope full of cash and leaned back against the door. There were more green bills than she could count with her eyes. Forgetting what she was doing and where she had to go, she sat at her kitchen table and counted the crisp one-hundred-dollar bills. Two, four, six.

Are there more? Eight, nine, ten. Ten one-hundred-dollar bills—a thousand dollars!

Where did this come from?

She stared at the money—the money she needed to pay rent, to have a home for Christmas. For Caroline to get her miracle.

Was this a miracle? Who sent this?

Her mother? No!

Really, delivery boy? You couldn't have delivered this money twenty minutes sooner? Of course you couldn't. You had to wait until after I had called my mother.

It wasn't her. Even she couldn't get money here that fast. And her message would have been, "Don't plan on me next month." She and the word miracle? It would take one for her to use it.

Was it Mrs. Shaw? She's generous, but she's saving all her money so she can visit her daughter.

The phone rang. *Oh, no—my interview!* She scrambled for her shoes and looked at the cash-filled envelope in her hand. She stashed it in the cabinet with the spices and ran for the door. She paused at the tree. Hadn't Caroline confessed to Papa about how they needed money for rent?

Miracles happen. Papa Shafer? Miracle trees? Could it have been him?

"Did you get the job?" Caroline asked.

"I don't know yet." Angela dodged her daughter's question. It was true—she didn't know for sure, but showing up fifteen minutes late did not convince the cafeteria manager she'd be reliable.

"When will you find out?"

"Don't know that either—maybe in a week. You didn't tell anyone at school, did you?"

Caroline grinned. "If I said, 'My mom might get a job here,' that's not lying, is it?"

"Caroline, I asked you not to. What if I don't get the job?" A question she didn't want to contemplate. "Let's do something else. Are you hungry for a snack? I'm sure we have celery." Angela opened the fridge.

"That's because you buy it and neither one of us eats it."

She was right. Easy meals and cheap food weren't the most nutritious, and occasionally Angela found herself strolling through the produce section for vegetables. Those shopping trips resulted in cauliflower, celery, or eggplant when it was on sale, food that sat in the fridge or on the counter until it was the last thing left to eat.

So far, Angela had been able to keep the mystery cash a secret from Caroline. She planned to investigate and find out if Papa Shafer or his grandson, Mark, had anything to do with it.

Of course they did. To pinpoint why this bothered her would require her to admit, at least to herself, that she didn't want their help, or that she was embarrassed to need it. Maybe she'd have to admit that she didn't want Mark thinking of her like that.

But he isn't thinking of me. He's thinking of someone named "Nat."

While they were in the middle of making cream cheese boats out of the celery, someone knocked on their door. They looked at each other, both with wide eyes—Angela's from dread, Caroline's from excitement.

"Stay here," Angela said as she crossed the kitchen to more knocking and opened the door.

"Are you Angela Donovan?" asked a man holding a microphone.

What in the world? "Yes."

"Good. I'm a reporter from WCGB, Channel 6 News," he said.

That's what his coat says, and that would explain the cameraman behind him.

"We understand you bought a tree from the Shafer Family Tree Farm. Is that correct?"

She glanced to her left and there it stood. "Yes, well, sort of." She didn't feel like explaining the whole "donated gift" part from the night before. She had tried to pay for it.

36

"And have you noticed anything different about it?"

"Not really."

"We heard there's something special about these trees. The people who buy them have unexpected things happen. We understand you received a generous gift after buying your tree."

Seriously? How could they know this? Am I under surveillance? Angela studied his logo. *And why is this news? Is this guy for real?*

"Mom, who is it?" Caroline grabbed her mom around the waist.

"Caroline, I said stay—" Angela glanced at the camera. "Is that thing on?"

"Yes. We can turn it off, but we'd like to know how you feel about the gift of money you received."

"What money?" Caroline asked.

Terrific! Now she knows. "How did you say you found out about that?"

He didn't hear her question. He was already asking the next one.

"Was it a miracle?"

With one arm on her daughter's shoulder, she opened her mouth, not knowing her answer.

CHAPTER 6

One conversation. Mark waited all weekend to find the time to have one ten-minute conversation with Papa. But there were customers to help, trees to cut and move, and the sales lot to prepare. Opening weekend by itself served as evidence that little else could compete with the work of the farm—never mind the rest of the year. How could Mark expect to work on his music as long as there was another tree to grow, another tree to sell?

Tuesday morning, Mark found Papa with Donna watching the news.

"I'm not an expert on miracles. I don't have an explanation for this, if that's what you mean." Mark recognized the woman on the screen—her dark, curly hair and pretty face.

The reporter summarized the story and said, "We contacted the Shafer Farm and asked what made their trees special. They said 'We take good care of the trees.' We'll have more about Shafer miracle trees later today. Back to you, Diane."

Mark shut off the TV and looked at Papa and Donna in disbelief.

That reporter never told me any of this.

"Land sakes," Papa said and slapped his knee. "This could be a problem."

"You're right," Mark said. "Do you know how many upset customers we'll have if they see this story?"

"That's not what I mean." Papa stood and folded his arms across his chest. "That reporter is telling *everybody* about our miracle trees, and that's not his place. You have to choose the right customers carefully."

"What are you talking about, Papa?"

"I haven't told you everything there is to being the keeper, but you should be able to understand that the customers who believe aren't disappointed."

More of Papa's stories. "Did you ask that reporter to feature us?" Mark asked, keeping his tone even.

"I sure didn't. What's done is done, though. I don't mind the publicity part of it—we can handle that. I'm more concerned for you—if you can figure out who you can and can't tell about the miracles," Papa said.

"This is the wrong kind of publicity," Mark said. "We'll get sued for false advertising if we don't put a stop to it."

"How are you going to do that? Come on now. Think about what's best for the trees—and the customers."

It wasn't adding up. Mark couldn't ignore Papa's earnest face and sincere voice. But if Papa didn't want to tell everyone about the trees, why would he contact a news station and talk to a reporter? Unless he didn't know he was talking to a reporter, or maybe he didn't know a reporter was listening. Mark looked at Donna.

"Papa's right," Donna said. "I don't think it's a coincidence. That woman has a Shafer tree in her home, and now she has money for rent."

"I knew she was a believer!" Papa said. "You see, you have to find the people with the light in their eye. Not the skeptical ones—no tree on the lot can help them. Of course, as you get some practice, you can tell the ones who are pretending to be skeptical, but deep down, they believe."

Mark sat down in the desk chair. Is this what Papa did? Size up customers; try to find some light in their eye? The phone rang.

"I'll answer it out front," Donna said, heading for the door.

"Papa, I'm not happy with our farm being used for the human interest story on Channel 6," Mark explained. "A few more customers can't hurt anything, but we'll have to be careful how much we talk about the trees and the miracles."

"That's my point," Papa said.

"Good. Then we're agreed." Mark said. *Doesn't have to be for the same reasons.* "I came to find you this morning so we could talk." He skipped his rehearsed introduction. "I'm ready."

Papa didn't answer and walked to the window.

"I'm ready to keep the trees." Mark clenched his jaw, John Jackson's offer and Natalie's ring clouding his mind.

"What makes you say that?" Papa's words were slow and deliberate.

"It's a gut feeling, Papa." He did have a feeling it was time to take over the farm, and a feeling to sell it while there was someone who would buy all the land.

"Do you know what makes the trees special?" Papa asked. "Why they can cause miracles?" He turned from the window and stared at Mark.

Mark got up from his chair, not expecting the question. He knew he needed to convince Papa he was ready, and that was all that mattered.

"You love these trees, and the people who buy them do too. That's enough for me. If there's something else that makes them special, even better," Mark said as he held Papa's gaze.

Mark waited for the twinges in his stomach to stop, for Papa to decide. He'd rather they agreed about the sale. He'd rather his father and mother were still alive, for that matter, so he wouldn't be in this position in the first place—trying to do what was best for Papa and the farm without anyone who could understand.

"Okay, then. That settles it. I'll call Ms. Dawson tomorrow. She can make it official," Papa said. "You've got a lot to learn, but I'm not getting any younger. It's about time you stepped up. What will you tell Natalie?"

"That I'm the new owner. She'll understand."

"What will you do about the news story?" Papa asked.

It sounded like a test question to Mark.

Maybe I shouldn't push my luck.

"I guess if the customers are happy, I don't have to do anything."

Papa's shoulders relaxed. "Good. I've been waiting for this day for a long time. Let's get to work out there."

"Do you mind if I tell Donna?" *And call Natalie and John Jackson?*

"Do what you need to do." Papa said.

Donna had left to go open the craft barn. Once Papa bundled up and walked outside, Mark returned to the office to make some calls.

I'll catch up with Donna later. And maybe the publicity isn't such a bad thing. At least our last season will be our best. We can go out on a high note.

When will I tell Papa? And what will I say?

Maybe I can sell all but the acres needed for Papa to keep his cabin. And maybe the craft barn for Donna?

The transfer of the farm ownership and the sale of it would take weeks to complete. It was premature to call his real estate agent, but Mark did it anyway. He arranged to meet at the house on Hickory Street in an hour.

Gray clouds covered most of the eastern sky, giving the farmhouse a spotted shadow cover in his rearview mirror. He looked at the porch steps before he turned out of the parking lot, the trees obscuring his view. He and his dad sat on those steps snapping beans in the summer when he was eight or nine years old. One time when his mom came out and reached for the beans, his dad pulled her onto his lap and they laughed, carefree and happy. The sound of their voices came to him like they were in a tunnel, their laughter moving further away, becoming harder to hear. Much of the farm served as a reminder of what he didn't have.

He called Natalie to plan a meeting at the house she hadn't seen yet.

"You sound excited. What's going on?" Natalie asked.

"Did you see the news about the tree farm?"

"No, what news?"

"Channel 6 did a story on a woman who bought one of our trees—a few days later, someone gave her money for rent. They're calling the trees miracle trees." Mark checked the road to make sure he didn't miss the exit.

"They ran a news story about miracle trees?" Natalie asked.

"Can you believe it? Hey, are you busy? I'm on my way to Hickory Street. Can I pick you up in five minutes?" he asked.

"Why?"

"To see the house," Mark said.

"The house?"

"Yeah, the house I'm trying to buy—the one with a music

studio. You've got to see it."

"Sounds fun, but we've got new inventory. I'm leaving for work early," she said.

"Are we still on for dinner tonight?" he asked.

"How about tomorrow?"

"Wow, you're that busy? Okay, let's plan for tomorrow."

After he finished his conversation with Natalie, Mark called John Jackson and left a message with his secretary to return the call. He pulled up to the house behind his real estate agent.

"Has business been good?" Mark asked as he pointed to the agent's new Jeep.

"Gotta have something for the snow," Dave answered. "Why the renewed interest in the house?" he asked Mark as they walked up to the door.

"I never lost interest."

They walked in through the screened-porch entry.

"It looks like these have all been winterized," Dave said, referring to the doors and windows.

Mark scanned the empty family room.

I could propose here. He glanced around to the kitchen, not having thoroughly looked at it the first time he toured the house. He walked over and opened a few cupboards, then leaned against the sink, folding his arms.

"How's your grandfather?" Dave asked.

"Good," Mark said. "How's Crystal? You two have been married, what, three years now?"

"Four. We're having a baby. Crystal's due in June," Dave said with a proud smile.

"Hey that's great. Congratulations!" Mark did his best to sound sincere. Four years and a baby. *At the rate I'm going, I'll look like my son's grandfather.*

Mark walked from room to room, looking at empty walls and judging how much furniture would fit. Back in the kitchen, he pictured dinner with Natalie in the dining area. He asked Dave about the owners.

"I checked today. No offers, but they are holding firm on the price," Dave said.

"Can we offer a little less and see what happens?"

"We can, but maybe I missed something. Did you say your financing is in place? Last time we talked, you said your grandfather might sell his farm. That hasn't happened yet, has it?" Dave walked over to the kitchen counter and tapped his fingers.

Sutton was too small and the tree farm too large for the sale of it to go unnoticed, especially by a real estate agent. Mark paced in the kitchen and answered cautiously. "Not yet."

"Look, Mark, no offense, but that's what you told me last month, and the month before that. Word is, John Jackson is doing everything he can to get your grandfather to sell—and Papa won't. So, what are we doing here? I mean, I don't mind bringing you by and letting you check the place out—dream a little—but unless you have another way to pay for it, we can't make an offer." Dave pulled out his phone and checked his messages.

Mark ran both hands through his hair.

Does Dave know everything John Jackson's doing? And who else knows? Maybe this was a bad idea.

"If I come up with enough for the down, say next week, could we do it then?" Mark asked.

"I'd love to do it for you, Mark. I would." Dave said after a minute. "This place is a gem—it's one of a kind. I know you're in love with the studio. Call your lender. They might be swamped this week with the end of the month and Christmas right around the corner. Then tell me what you want to do."

Was that pity in Dave's voice, or impatience? He always sounded busy, maybe a little rushed, but did he feel sorry for Mark?

"I'm not trying to waste your time, Dave. I think I have a way to do this. I should be able to make an offer in a week. How does that sound?"

"One week is fine. There aren't too many people in Sutton looking for a recording studio in their basement, so you should be okay. Let me know." Dave didn't look convinced. "Is your grandfather seriously planning to sell the farm? Where is he going to live? Is he looking for a place?" Ever the real estate agent.

Mark cringed. Why hadn't they walked out of the house sooner? How could he answer? How could Mark explain that Papa wasn't selling the farm—*he* was? Or that Papa didn't want to live anywhere else, and he certainly wasn't looking for a new home because he didn't have any idea yet that he might need one? It was the last detail of Mark's plan that wasn't worked out yet. He hadn't talked it over with John Jackson, but he hoped to sell all but a few acres to allow Papa to remain in his cabin. What were a few acres out of fifty?

"No, he's not looking." Mark paused. "I'm not sure what he'll do."

"He's not thinking of living with your sister in LA, is he? I can't picture him anywhere else but on your farm. Remember how after our basketball games, we'd go over to your place and he'd let us ride the—"

"I remember. Yeah, good times." It was abrupt to cut Dave off like that, but Mark needed to get back to the farm, and more reminiscing could lead to more probing. "I've got to run. Thanks, Dave. I'll call you next week."

Mark headed back to the farm. *Dave* would *bring up Kate.* December was about the time she would call and explain her production schedule, how flying home for Christmas would interfere. She worked for a small film company and always had a reason why she couldn't leave, even for a few days.

Usually they had the least amount of traffic at the tree farm on weekdays. For families that traveled from other parts of Massachusetts, the weekends were the best days to make the drive. Mark rounded the corner to the farm and hit the brakes. An unexpected line of cars funneled into the parking lot.

Mark carefully navigated a U-turn over the gravel and took the private road that circled the farm and brought him to Papa's cabin. He walked over to the office from there. Donna waved him down while holding the phone to her ear.

Could this be because of Channel 6? So much for a quiet Tuesday afternoon.

"Where have you been?" Donna demanded. "We need to call in our temporary employees. These phones keep ringing, and I need to get back to the register. Are you staying here, or helping Papa on the lot?"

"I'd better leave the phones to the expert." He motioned to her. "I'll help Papa. Are these customers here to buy miracle trees?"

"What do *you* think?" Donna threw her hands in the air.

Mark found Papa outside on the sales lot. They worked for hours with a near-steady stream of friendly customers.

Mark called in some extra employees and checked on Donna to see if she needed any more help. She didn't get flustered very often—she could handle opening weekend and be even more energized when it was over. She had told Mark that the farm was easier to manage since they had scaled back after his parents died. They had stopped offering pictures with Santa and had also closed the small reindeer village.

"Is everything going okay here?" Mark asked.

"We're doing fine. I'll call some of my crafters and tell them about our increased demand," Donna said. "What did you and Papa talk about this morning?"

Mark dodged the question. "Thanks for keeping things under control."

Donna persisted. "Let me guess—it's you and Natalie. I haven't said a word, but Papa's been asking me every time I turn around if you two are going to 'settle down', as he calls it."

"No, that's not it. She and I—we might be, but I still have to ask her." Mark's face burned red.

"Tell me later, then. I like to hear good news," she said before she greeted another customer at the register. Mark agreed, relieved that she was too busy to continue that conversation.

I'll have to find the right time to tell her.

On his way back outside, Mark's cell phone rang.

"Hello?"

"John Jackson here. Is this Shafer?" he asked.

"Yes, this is Mark."

"I saw the news today. Are you out of your mind? Are you trying to kill this deal?" John demanded.

"What? No. I left you a message to tell you that we're—that I'm ready to negotiate. My grandfather is transferring ownership of the farm to me, and I'd like to sell."

"Is that right? Well, you'll need to do something about this nuisance of a publicity stunt. Make it go away, Mark," John demanded.

"What do you mean?"

"Tell me something, how many customers do you have at your farm today? How many of those customers are going to like my client if he puts an auto mall on your land?"

Now it's an auto mall? Mark didn't answer.

"Make this go away, like yesterday, or we won't have a deal."

CHAPTER 7

Angela stopped answering her phone less than a day after the news story aired. She was no longer in the mood to explain to another curious acquaintance if it was true—the tree and the anonymous gift of money. And she was avoiding the call from the person she least wanted to speak to—Mr. Buckley.

Not that he could apply any more pressure than her daughter had. From the moment Caroline learned about the money, she had declared it their Christmas miracle and begged her mother to pay the rent as soon as the office opened.

"It's December first, Mom, and we can stay for the month and then you'll get a job."

"Technically, we have a three-day grace period. We don't have to pay today," Angela explained.

"Why wouldn't we?" Caroline was clearly baffled.

"I've got to figure some things out. Don't worry about it."

After Angela dropped Caroline off at school, she returned home and called Mrs. Shaw.

"I think the Shafer family is using me," she complained.

"I'm not sure what you mean."

"It's wrong. They are using me, or what happened to me, for publicity instead of paying for a real ad campaign or something."

Angela loaded the dishwasher while they talked.

"Are you talking about Channel 6? I saw that story," Mrs. Shaw said. "Well, there have been other miracles. Today a family found their lost dog after buying a tree, and then there was the man whose car started working again. It looks like you aren't the only one."

"I'm the only one who had a specific amount of cash brought to her door. It had to be them," Angela insisted. "They created that 'miracle' and sent a reporter so they could take credit for it—and apparently all the other good things happening in Sutton. I feel used, and I don't like it."

"That sounds unlikely, dear—a bit fantastic. I know the family. Well, I know Donna—she runs the craft barn at the farm, and they sell my crafts there. It doesn't sound like something they'd do," Mrs. Shaw said. "What have you done with the money?"

"I haven't done anything with it. It's sitting in my spice cabinet," Angela said.

"Do you realize you're being terribly suspicious of a good thing in your life?"

Angela absorbed that comment like a full sponge.

"Today is the first, Angela. Has it occurred to you to pay your rent and be grateful? Even if the tree farm created the story by giving you that money, they can't ask for it back."

Angela stopped moving, the water running over a plate needlessly.

"Oh that's an idea, Mrs. Shaw!"

"What did I say?"

"You helped me figure out what to do."

Angela left the plate in the sink, dried her hands, and grabbed the envelope and her coat. The truck refused to start for a full five minutes, but she persisted. Halfway to the tree farm, she checked her gas gauge and did a quick calculation to make sure she'd have enough gas to get home.

That's all I'd need next is to get stranded out there.

There were plenty of spaces in the parking lot—it wasn't even ten in the morning yet. She turned off the truck and pulled the money from her purse. She counted it one more time.

Open or not, I'm going in.

But she didn't knock.

She heard a chopping sound, ax to wood. She stepped over to

the end of the porch and saw Mark Shafer with his back to her splitting a log. The crackling sound cut through the chill morning air. She stood for a moment, mouth ajar, watching his shoulders move. He swung again, full of force, yet so precise.

Why couldn't she take her eyes off of him?

What's the matter with me? It's not like I haven't seen a man chopping wood before, right? Well at least not in person. Okay, never.

Mark paused and allowed the ax to rest at his side while he wiped his brow. Angela stepped back to the front door. Deep breaths, she took deep breaths and tried to remember what she was doing there at the farmhouse in the first place.

She knocked on the hand-carved wooden door. A middle-aged woman opened the door and greeted her with a friendly face.

"We don't open for another hour. Can I help you with something?"

"I have a return," Angela said. The woman stared at her. Angela tried to clarify. "I mean, I have something to give back."

"Do you mean one of our trees, or something from the craft barn?"

"No, not a tree."

Although, that's an idea . . .

"Here, please come in," the woman said. She opened the door wider and stepped out of the way.

Morning light streamed through a front window of the farmhouse. Angela smelled an omelet cooking, though she couldn't see a kitchen.

"I need to talk to someone about some money . . . I think belongs to you."

The woman tilted her head and then said, "Wait here, and let me find Mark."

He was already coming through the back door, pulling off his gloves. "Oh, hey there," he said.

"Mark, this woman wants to talk to you about a return."

"Sorry, I've been out chopping firewood." He said.

"I noticed, I mean—how nice. Um, no problem." *Really, I can't complete a sentence?*

"Come over here," he said, motioning to the counter. "It's good to see you, Mrs. . . . uh, Mrs. . . . what was your name again?"

She walked over to where he stood at the cash register.

"Angela Donovan. It's not Mrs.," she answered, instantly

chiding herself for making that last point.

Like it matters to him if I'm married. Why does he have to be so good-looking?

She held the envelope of money in her hand tighter.

Mark repeated her name. "Were you . . . on the news?"

Angela shifted her weight and took a deep breath. She looked at the older woman and back at Mark.

"About that." She lifted the envelope of cash to the counter, but didn't release it from her grip. "I'm returning this. I didn't ask for it, and I can't accept it. It would be better if you took it back." She watched their faces register surprise.

Was Mrs. Shaw right? Do I sound unappreciative?

"Take it back? I can't do that," he said.

"I'm not ungrateful," she continued, "but it isn't right to give someone money as a way to get publicity." The words were harder to say than she had imagined.

Mark tapped his fingers on the counter and didn't respond.

The older woman spoke first. "Honey, we didn't give you that money."

"She's right," Mark agreed. "I don't know where that money came from, but if I did, it would explain a few things around here."

"So I suppose you didn't call the news station, either?" Angela asked as she became more uncomfortable.

"No, we didn't. In fact, we'd like to find out who did. It's created kind of a problem for us," Mark answered.

"It's a problem to have free advertising and eager customers?" Angela responded. This wasn't going the way she'd planned. She looked down at the envelope.

"If that *were* my money," he said, "I'd take it back. Wait—what I mean to say is if I had given it to you, I *could* take it back, but if you really needed it, I wouldn't. I'd want you to have it."

"What?" Angela asked, not able to follow his logic—or lack of it. "Um, never mind. I'll go." She lifted the money off the counter. "I'm sorry." Bewildered, she turned to leave.

"Thanks for coming," Mark called as she walked out the door.

The older woman said something to him, but she couldn't hear her exact words.

She walked back to the parking lot, now filling up with other cars. Papa Shafer's words returned to her mind like the swirling wind. "Special trees," he'd called them. "Miracle trees . . . believe," he'd told her. If they hadn't given her that money to get some extra press, then who had? Did it matter? Was it a miracle? Did it have anything to do with Shafer trees?

She focused on what she did know: someone learned that she needed money, and they gave it to her. She couldn't give it back.

As she pulled out of the lot, she looked at the festively decorated porch of the farmhouse. Sunlight highlighted the tops of trees lined up waiting for a home. A longing formed inside her—what was it? Homesickness? But her upscale home in Providence was nothing like this. Father's career required an image. This was a craving for land, the farm—for belonging. The way Mark and that woman worked together and the warmth in their home.

Or was it a longing for something more—maybe for Mark? He'd seen her on the news, asked her name. Did he mean to ask Miss or Mrs.? And something else surprised her. He didn't have some of the expressions she expected to see if he were hiding something—the down-turned eyes and pulled-back smile of someone relieved to be found out, or the mock humility of someone who was glad they'd been caught doing a good thing. It was even sweet, the way he had fumbled over his words when he tried to explain that he couldn't take the money. Frustrating, but sweet.

I have no idea where this money came from, and no one's stopping me from using it to pay the rent. I'll do this for Caroline. We can have a home for Christmas. And maybe I'll have time to find a job.

She drove around to the apartment office to pay the rent.

"Hey, good morning, Angie," Mr. Buckley said as soon as he saw her.

"Hi, Mr. Buckley, I'd like to pay the rent for December *and* what I owe for November."

It does feel good to say that.

"I've been thinking about you. You look as pretty on TV as you do in person. That's something else about those trees! There are a few other tenants who could use a tree like that—if they really are miracle trees, that is." He chuckled.

Angela pulled the money from her purse as quickly as she could. Any conversation with Mr. Buckley caused her stomach to turn. He had to be at least fifteen years her senior and twice divorced, points he emphasized often.

"The trees are nice, but—"

"Boy, I'm glad you're sticking around. Before I saw you on the news, I had this idea. I couldn't imagine evicting you and your daughter in December, of all the months. I was thinking that the office can be busy and it would be nice to have a little help here. So I was thinking of you."

I'm walking out if he tells me he was thinking of me one more time.

"Would you like a part-time job here? We can call it 'assistant office manager'." He looked at her expectantly.

"Thank you, Mr. Buckley, but . . ." *Quick, think of something.* "I've interviewed at the school and I'll be starting in January." She looked away and almost dropped the envelope of money. She started counting bills.

I'm a terrible liar!

"Here," she said.

"The school, huh? That's too bad. I mean, no, that's great," he said as he took her money. "Even if you could work here, say, a few hours a week, that would help."

Is he serious?

"Wait," she said. "Shouldn't I pay by check or money order?"

"Don't worry about it. I can work that out." He slid the money into a desk drawer.

Angela bit her lip and wished she could hit a rewind button. "Can I get a receipt?" She didn't like asking him for anything.

"You don't need one, but sure, I'll find the book. Have a seat."

I'll stand, thanks.

Angela returned to her apartment with the receipt in hand, not sure what to make of the day. Somehow after she had embarrassed herself at the tree farm and declined a questionable job offer from Mr. Buckley, she'd lost the fleeting good feeling of having her rent paid in full. At least Caroline would be happy.

Angela picked up a few things at the grocery store and they celebrated by baking Caroline's favorite cupcakes. Caroline announced there were fourteen more days of school and asked what kind of fun things they could do together over the break. Then she asked her mother what gift she'd like for Christmas, a question Angela had deliberately avoided until now.

"Christmas came early for us," Angela said. "You don't have to worry about giving me a gift. What about you? What do you want this year?"

"An Easy Bake Oven, with the special mixes," she said.

That's doable.

"And a big family dinner," Caroline continued.

"A what? We don't have a big family!" Angela exclaimed.

We have a family with a big gap in it is more like it. Once Todd remarried and then moved to Florida, staying connected meant that Caroline received a card for the holiday—on time, if she were lucky.

Angela smoothed frosting over the next several cupcakes, proving to herself that it was easier for her to sugarcoat a cupcake than the not-so-sweet-parts of their family life.

She finished cleaning up the kitchen after Caroline went to sleep and then she settled herself into bed. As she drifted off to sleep, the phone rang.

"Hello? Who is this?" Angela whispered.

"Your mother. Who else calls you at this time of night?"

No one. I should have guessed. "What's wrong?" Angela asked.

"I drove to Sutton today—that's what's wrong," her mother said. "I met your landlord. He seems quite fond of you."

Angela had to sit up to make sure she was even hearing her correctly.

"Caroline is sleeping, so what did you say about my landlord? Why did you drive here?"

"To pay your rent—today *is* the first. Imagine how silly I felt when your landlord explained that you had already paid your rent today."

"Oh, no—I forgot to tell you. I'm sorry."

"Would it have been too hard to call me? Maybe *before* I drove all the way out there?" her mother continued.

"I would have called, but I didn't know I was going to pay rent today," Angela whispered.

"For heaven's sakes, that doesn't make any sense. How could you not know you were going to pay your rent?"

"I said I'm sorry. Did you see the news report? Can I call you tomorrow to explain?"

"No, I'm fine. Don't bother," her mother said and hung up.

Angela tossed and turned. Her mother had driven to Sutton, tried to pay rent, and had a *lovely* conversation with Mr. Buckley.

Mrs. Catherine Elliott could not be fine.

CHAPTER 8

Mark spent the remainder of Tuesday night and all day Wednesday downplaying the news story to customers. John Jackson's call the day before had put him on edge. How was he supposed to "make it go away?" He was eager instead to share the change in ownership news with Natalie.

The lot finally emptied and Donna asked him to help clean up in the craft barn. That meant she expected to talk. He sent a message to Natalie, asking if they could meet at the restaurant as he wouldn't have as much time to pick her up.

"Did you sell out of anything tonight?" Mark asked.

"Mrs. Shaw's cranberry wreaths—she won't tell me how she makes them. Not that I could do the kind of detail work she does."

"That's not too bad, considering the crowd we had here. Speaking of the crowd, what can we do about the news? You know the farm better than I do, but please tell me you can see how this could be trouble. It's tacky, at the very least."

"Maybe it was a slow news day. For better or worse, all this fuss will die down when there's another headline. I wouldn't worry about it," Donna said. "More importantly, what has Papa smiling and your brow furrowed?"

Mark opened a new box of inventory.

She'll find out soon enough—it might as well be from me.

"Papa called Ms. Dawson today. I'm taking ownership of the farm," he said as he lined the shelf with evergreen boughs.

Donna put down the mistletoe ornaments she held. "Mark, I'm glad to hear that. Papa isn't the only one around here that thinks you're the best man for the trees."

Mark didn't look up. Her sincerity, instead of smooth and comforting, pricked his heart like tree needles under his nails.

"No wonder he's happy," she continued. "What a relief! I admit I've been worried about you and Natalie after our last conversation. I thought for sure she had convinced you to quit. Does she know yet?"

"I'm telling her at dinner. And she hasn't convinced me of anything." Mark made that point clear. "She's not as bad as everyone thinks, you know."

"Not bad, Mark, just not right for you. But I suppose that if she loves you, she'll learn to love the farm."

"Donna, do you have any idea how many women want to marry a man who's already married to a tree farm? I'll tell you. Zero. Ask me how I know."

The relief on Donna's face changed to concern again. "Any woman who loves you will accept what you love. She won't ask you to choose." She picked up the mistletoe again. "And if you love her, you'll give her the chance to know you, to love everything about you."

Was she right? Had he even given Natalie that chance? He shook his head at the thought. He still had his music, and Papa wasn't getting any younger.

The next words didn't form as easily. How could he help her understand that selling the farm was for the best?

"Donna, I'm planning to—"

"We have so much to talk about—I have a lot to tell you. Your mom and dad shared things with me that I'm not sure even Papa remembers. If you had up and quit, I would have figured something out, but I'm so glad you're staying," she said. "Come here. I need to give you a big hug."

Mark stood and moved the empty box with his foot. Donna rushed over and gave him one of her signature squeezes. "Your mother would be so happy right now."

"You don't have to say that." Memories of his mother and

father clouded his mind. "I was trying to say . . ." He couldn't finish.

"I'm sorry. No one can take her place—I shouldn't try to speak for her. But she would be proud of you, I'm sure of it."

Proud of me?

"I've got to go." Mark stepped back and picked up the box for something to do. He glanced at his watch and then at the door. The craft barn had never felt so small and suffocating.

"Any chance you can cancel your dinner with Natalie? I'm not kidding when I say I've got a lot to tell you about this farm."

"She's at the restaurant by now. Let's talk another night," he said.

Mark took a deep breath of the December night air as he walked to his car, cold but refreshing. He wiped the sweat off his forehead and looked over his shoulder to the back lot of trees.

The trees are quiet tonight.

Wait—what?

Before sitting in his car, he brushed off the side of his pant leg covered in glitter from the craft barn.

What does Donna know, and why did she have to bring up my mother and father tonight?

He waited at the red light and changed the track on his CD, increasing the volume too. Not that it mattered. Donna's words echoed louder. *Would my mother be proud? And if my dad were still alive? All of this would be pointless. He and Mom would be running the farm side by side like Papa and Nana.*

Mark pulled into the parking lot of the restaurant. Though Nana had been gone some years now, his stomach lurched at the thought of her meeting Natalie. *She would not approve.*

"I'm relieved to see you," Mark said as he approached the table where Natalie sat.

"What took you so long?"

"Customers and Donna—she wanted to talk," he said. "It's amazing what one little news story can do. At least sales will be up."

"Did your grandfather orchestrate that? Is he that worried about selling the farm?" she asked with a new accusatory tone.

"No, Papa had nothing to do with it. We have no idea how it started," he said, thinking about the last two days. "He doesn't know I'm planning to sell, either, so no, that's not it. The strange thing is that the woman who received the money—the one on the news? She showed up at the farm today and tried to give it back!"

"What? Why would she do that?"

"That's my point. She thought we had something to do with the news story too."

"Wait—is this the same girl with the old truck you helped last week, and she came back today?" Natalie asked in an even harsher tone. "Did she ask for you?"

"No. I mean, yes, it was the same girl, but she didn't ask for me. I happened to be there, but so was Donna." Mark leaned back in his chair and picked up the menu, using it as a shield.

"I already ordered for you."

What's with her?

Mark eyed Natalie and closed the menu. "Thanks. Do you want to hear my good news? Or did you order the food to go?" he asked, not hiding his annoyance.

"Sorry. We have a new regional manager. She wasn't in the store five minutes before she had changed our holiday floor plan. Do you know what that means?" She continued berating the manager and complaining about work until the food arrived and she wound down.

Mark couldn't wait any longer. "Papa is transferring ownership of the farm. To me."

Natalie looked up from her plate. "Are you serious? When?"

"He made the call today. I don't know how long it will take to make it legal. But as far as Papa is concerned, it's official. You're looking at the new owner of the Shafer Tree Farm." Mark straightened in his seat.

Natalie reached across the table and took one of his hands. She looked sincerely happy. "You've known this all day and let me go on and on, complaining about the store?"

Mark felt his pocket, where the ring still waited. "I wanted to tell you in person. I saw the house yesterday too."

"That's right. How did that go?"

"Great. I'm planning to make an offer on it next week. I'd love for you to see it."

"I can't believe it has a music studio in the basement. That will be great for you," she said.

For us. It will be great for us.

They finished dinner, and Mark hugged Natalie by her car after they left the restaurant. Mark assured her that when the holiday season ended, they'd have more time to celebrate. He drove home, and in his bedroom at the back of the farmhouse, he found some of his old CDs he'd recorded when he was just out of high school. It was late, and he could feel the number of trees he had lifted in the tightness of his shoulders. A new song played through his mind.

He pulled out a yellow legal pad and wrote one verse of a new melody, then a chorus. He looked at the picture of his parents on a shelf in his bedroom. They were standing together outside—near some trees, of course. He set down his notepad, walked over, and picked up the picture. Didn't he have it memorized? Would looking at it again give him any more information about his parents that he didn't already have? His father's arm was draped loosely around his mother's shoulders; she held a canvas purse with a large sunflower print on it. He knew her smile, too—soft and content. Mark held the picture close and scrutinized his mother's hands. He looked at her left hand to find the ring on her finger. He could make out the band and the stone, but the shape and size were grainy. He set the picture down, disappointed—it was too much like his memories, missing the finer details.

He pulled out a box from under his bed and rummaged through some papers. Donna helped him collect whatever they could find in those early days after the fire. There were some pictures and other pieces of their life. He sifted through the irrelevant material, like utility bills, and sorted the pictures into groups—one pile before he was born, another for later. He thumbed through them, avoiding the heavy feeling that stirred in his heart when he did this. He had been through this box enough times to know it did not contain what he was looking for—a picture of his parents someplace other than the farm.

He put away the box and looked out his bedroom window over the thick pines that stretched for miles behind the house.

They left plenty of trees.

Mark returned to his legal pad of paper and reread what he'd written of the new song, words of love and dreams and what it takes to make them come true.

The verse and chorus don't match. Something isn't right.

CHAPTER 9

Angela grabbed her sweatshirt, pulled on her slippers and a pair of gloves, and peeked out of the window. Several inches of snow had fallen overnight. She would have slept longer to avoid the frosty apartment air if not for Caroline's exuberance.

"Snow day! Is school cancelled? Mom, you look funny like that. How much snow did we get?"

"The sky is clear and the road looks fine too," she said.

"Then can we do something fun after school?" Caroline asked.

"We made cupcakes last night. What did you have in mind?" Angela pulled on her boots.

"Let's go Christmas shopping!"

"Hold on—I'm going grocery shopping today. Food before presents." Angela listened to herself. Always putting on the brakes. "We could make gingerbread cookie ornaments? We'll use Grandma Elliott's recipe."

More like her housekeeper's recipe . . .

"Can I roll the dough?" Caroline asked.

"Sure, after you finish your homework."

After returning home from taking Caroline to school, Angela sorted through her mail and lined up the bills that she needed to pay. She had a message from the school cafeteria manager to come in at four o'clock that afternoon for a second interview.

Angela called Mrs. Shaw and asked if Caroline could stay with her for the short time she'd be gone. She also told her what had happened at the tree farm, and how she ended up using the money to pay her rent.

"I'm glad to hear it. We never know why things happen the way they do," Mrs. Shaw said. "I'm glad that it's settled."

"Me too," Angela agreed.

What was this light and airy feeling creeping over her? The rent paid and the school job a possibility—was this optimism? Or was it the Mrs. Shaw effect?

She's so different from my mother.

Oh, that's right—Mother!

She picked up the phone, and like she was prone to do when possessed of a cheerful spirit, she dialed herself right back into the fray.

"What do you say, Mom?" Angela asked assertively. "Do you want to come over tonight and make gingerbread cookie ornaments with us?" The invitation was a little random, but sincere.

"Tonight?" her mother asked. "I was just there yesterday."

"I feel bad about that—that's why I'm calling. Caroline has asked about you. She knows we use your recipe. Could we try to get along," Angela spoke carefully now, "for Caroline? It would be great if you came for her."

"What do you mean, 'try to get along'? We'd get along better if you didn't ask me to pay your rent when it had already been paid."

"I can explain that. I didn't know someone was going to give me money," Angela said.

"Who gave you money? How much did they give you?" her mother demanded.

"I don't know who. That's my point. I called you before that happened."

Here we go again.

"Is this money from a boyfriend? Because if it is, I hope you know that is *the worst*, and I mean the *worst* thing you could do—accept money from a boyfriend."

"No. I don't have a boyfriend, Mom. The money was an anonymous gift. I'm sure that's why I forgot to call. It was unexpected," Angela said.

Maybe this was a bad idea.

"Anyway, if you want to join us, we'll be making cookies tonight," Angela offered one more time and waited. Did the moment of silence before her mother answered mean she was softening?

"The roads will be ice, but I'll try to come," her mother finally said.

Angela wasn't sure if the cafeteria manager was giving her another chance or if it was routine to have a second interview for part-time work. Either way, she was grateful. She dropped off Caroline at Mrs. Shaw's early and arrived at the school on time.

She was given more paperwork to fill out and was introduced to some of the staff. The manager explained that she had to wait for final approval before she could give her a start date, but as far as she was concerned, Angela had the job. She handed her the schedule for upcoming training days and finished showing her around the kitchen.

Where was the relief she expected to feel at this job offer? A job, a paycheck—what was the problem? Only that Angela never imagined she'd need to work two jobs to make ends meet, never thought they'd come so close to eviction if not for some mysterious gift. There was a time when she was married to Todd that her music recordings sold for good money. But that was years ago, eons in the music industry. Younger, trendier musicians had claimed that space now.

At least there was one person she was excited to tell.

Angela reached for her phone, but left it in her purse. No use calling when she'd be home in less than ten minutes and could see Caroline's face when she heard the news in person.

The low-lying road wound around to the entrance of her apartment. The sky loomed darker above her, but trees blocked her view of the buildings. Those weren't storm clouds—what were they? She pulled into the entrance, but a policeman stood in the parking lot. He held up one hand and motioned for her to turn around. Confused, she watched him for a moment. She put her truck in reverse and backed up. Now she saw at least three fire trucks outside the apartment building.

Why are there fire trucks?

Then she saw them—flames devouring the roof. She gasped, held her breath, and watched the thick, black smoke swirl upward, filling the sky.

No, no, no. Caroline. Where is Caroline?

She fumbled out of the truck, leaving it in the street with the door open. She climbed over the snow mounds and the low parking lot wall, dropping into the snow on the other side. She picked herself up, ran straight for her stairwell, and screamed Caroline's name. Two firefighters stopped her. One on each side lifted her off the ground by the arms. Her feet kicked the air as they carried her behind a truck and put her down.

"We've gotten everyone out," they said.

"Where is my daughter? Caroline—she's eight. Oh, what was she wearing today? Was it a blue sweater?" Angela's heart pounded.

One fireman looked at the other and knelt down beside her.

"They've taken her to County Medical for smoke inhalation," he said evenly. Angela started crying and tried to stand. The fireman put his hand on her shoulder.

"We'll find someone to take you to her. Stay here for a few minutes," he said and walked over to one of the police officers.

Angela put her face in her hands.

Please let her be okay. I can't lose her. I can't.

Yells from other firefighters competed with the commotion of residents, families, and news reporters. She glanced up. The fire truck obscured her view of the building, but she could see the smoke billow heavenward, slow and dreamlike. The sky looked like it had been draped in gray, the trees, too. Or like a picture drained of color. The world, her world, drained of life.

Where is she? Where is Caroline? Please, please. Oh, let her be safe.

The fireman returned. "Officer McGrath will take you to see your daughter."

"What happened to her? What should I do with my truck?" Her scattered words tumbled out of her. She looked over and saw another policeman behind the wheel of it, moving it out of the street.

I must have left the key in the ignition.

"Travis will follow us. Come with me," Officer McGrath said. "It sounds like they took your daughter in for observation. Was she with her grandmother?"

"No, that's our neighbor. She was babysitting. Wait, is Mrs.

Shaw okay? What happened?"

"We're not sure—it could have been a candle. Three apartments were involved, but they've evacuated that entire unit over there."

Angela looked where the officer motioned to see her apartment building included in the evacuation.

Now what will we do?

The officers escorted Angela all the way to Caroline's room and returned the truck key before they left. A nurse offered to find the doctor. Angela held her hand over her mouth when she saw Caroline's ash-filled hair and sooty cheeks.

"Mom." Caroline whispered from under the oxygen mask.

Angela grabbed her hand and hugged her. She put her head as close to her little shoulders. "Are you okay?"

"The lamb. The little lamb." Caroline started to cry.

"Shh, it's okay. What's wrong?" Angela asked, bewildered.

"The lamb. Please don't be mad at me, Mom." Caroline coughed. "I took the lamb, the one from your nativity set, to Mrs. Shaw's today. When her apartment filled with smoke, the firefighters came to help us get out. I don't know what happened to it. I grabbed it, but it isn't in my pocket."

"It's okay, Caroline," Angela said. "Don't worry about the lamb. You're safe and we're together. That's all that matters."

"What if I lost the lamb?" Caroline cried.

"We can find a new one. Please don't worry."

Angela reassured her daughter, "Everything would be okay." She told her.

But would it? She looks okay, but what if she's not?

The doctor spoke to Angela in the hallway. He was kind and calm as he explained she hadn't suffered any burns—only smoke inhalation. They planned to run some tests and keep her overnight for observation.

"Do you have any questions?" he asked.

Of course I have questions. Like, are you sure she'll be okay? And what about the bill I'm going to get from the hospital—and you? How am I going to pay for it all? And why am I thinking about another bill at a time like this? What kind of a mother am I? Is our apartment ruined? And you look too young to be a doctor.

Tears welled up in Angela's eyes and spilled out, like they were making room for the converging flood of emotion and thought.

She shook her head, wiped her tears, and uttered something resembling "Thank you." With watery eyes, she watched the doctor walk away, his white coat and the hospital walls blurring together into a strange, surreal scene.

How could this be happening?

She returned to the room. Caroline had fallen asleep. Angela sat in the boxy, vinyl recliner next to the hospital bed, pulled her legs up to her chest, and watched her daughter. The low, humming sounds of the monitors and IV pump were a relief from the commotion of a few hours earlier. The whiteboard across from Caroline's bed had her name written on it and the name of her nurse and doctor. There was a calendar on the wall, the kind with one page for each day. NOV 30, it read. Angela pulled out her phone and checked the day. December 2nd.

I thought so. Oh, to go back.

Angela heard a slight knock on the wide hospital room door. She sat up, and her mother walked in.

"Mom!" She jumped up. Without speaking, her mother walked over and hugged her. *Was her mother crying?* She couldn't see. Angela buried her head into her mother's shoulder as the tears welled up again. It may have been years since they'd hugged like this, but leave it to Caroline to bring them together.

It's been so long. Don't cry. Not now.

Caroline stirred in the bed. Angela whispered, "She's okay— she's going to be fine. They're running tests."

"Thank goodness. What happened? What about you?" her mother asked.

Angela swallowed hard. "I'm fine. I wasn't there when the fire broke out. Caroline was with our neighbor. Her place filled with smoke because of another apartment where someone left candles burning or something—they aren't sure. Anyway, she's here for observation."

"I've never been so scared. I drove up to your place and it looked like a scene from the apocalypse, with the charred building and debris everywhere. Even the snow around the place was black. It took me forever to find someone who could tell me where you were," her mother said as she held on to one of Angela's arms. "I'm so relieved you're safe."

"Why did you come? How did you get here?" Angela couldn't decide what was more surprising—to see her mother in person, or to be hugged by her.

"I came to bake ornament cookies. Remember, you called this morning?"

"That's right—that's what Caroline wanted to do tonight." Angela looked at her daughter resting in the bed. "And you came." Angela looked at her mother and fought back more tears.

"Yes, and I'm glad I did. I'm not as cold-hearted as you think I am," her mother said and sat down in a chair. She pulled out her phone and dialed.

"Who are you calling?" Angela asked.

"Hello, Holly?" her mother said into the phone. "When you arrive at the house tomorrow, will you make up the beds in the doll room and the study? Yes, that's right. Thank you."

"Mom, what are you doing?"

"I'm getting things ready for you and Caroline to come and stay. What does it sound like I'm doing?"

Angela held the sides of her head with her hands. "But why?" She sat back into the recliner.

"You have to have someplace to live. This has gone on long enough."

Caroline stirred in the bed and the monitor slipped off her finger. Angela hopped up and fixed it while figuring out what to make of her mother's offer. She considered it for ten seconds.

"Thank you. That's generous of you, Mom, but we'll find a place in Sutton." She said as emphatically as her whisper would allow.

Her mother put her phone back in her designer purse. "I see. You won't ever come back, will you? Are you waiting for me to say I'm sorry? Is that it? As I was driving over here, I had no idea how seriously you, or Caroline, had been hurt. I care you know, I do."

Angela heard the emotion in her mother's voice, the catch in her throat. She looked to see the glint of tears in her eyes, her features full of concern. What was this? Love? Or something close to it?

What can I do?

"It's not that, Mom. Caroline has school."

She looked back to her sleeping daughter's face, her mother's emotion too much to process. No matter that just that morning, Angela had been the one to ask if they could try to get along. That was before the fire. Before she'd been scared out of her mind at the thought of losing Caroline. All she needed was for Caroline to be okay. Going home with her mother was not the answer.

CHAPTER 10

Mark had just finished his third mile on the treadmill when the morning news started. He watched the muted screen as it flashed scenes of a fire. He grabbed the remote for volume without taking his eyes from the report. He kept a steady pace until he couldn't stop the adrenaline rush. His legs pounded the belt harder, faster.

No. Not a fire, not in December.

Families huddled in the parking lot and firefighters worked to extinguish the blaze. Mark scanned the scene for children, out of habit. There were a few but he couldn't see any faces. The camera panned to the flames and then the station went to a commercial break.

Mark stopped the treadmill and grabbed his towel. He showered and ate breakfast before Donna arrived at the farm.

"What are you up to today?" she asked. "Big day with Natalie or something?"

"She's busy with work. Did you see the news this morning?" Mark asked as he shuffled papers on his desk.

"Did they feature us again?"

"No. There was a fire at the Blackstone Apartments yesterday."

"Goodness, that's where Mrs. Shaw lives. I hope she's okay,"

Donna said. "How bad was it?" She took off her coat and tied on her Christmas apron.

"There were three apartments involved in the fire, but they evacuated the building and another nine units. That's a lot of people who need to find a place to sleep." Mark searched on his computer for phone numbers.

"I'll try to reach Mrs. Shaw. What are you planning?"

"I want to use my mom's hospital fund. This is the kind of situation where she would have helped, don't you think?" Mark looked to Donna for confirmation.

"Oh, I think so. If she knew whole families were out of their homes, she wouldn't sit around."

Papa and Brett came into the office.

"Who wouldn't sit around?" Papa asked.

"My mom—we're talking about the fire. Did you see the news?"

Mark explained the details again as Donna hurried out.

"I'm calling the Red Cross to make a donation to help with temporary housing. I'm also donating trees for each family, too, once they're in a new place. Is that okay with you?" Mark asked.

"Okay with me? Course it is. Besides, you're taking care of the trees now, right? I think it's a fine idea. If there's anything those people need, it's a Shafer miracle tree."

Mark cringed. "Papa, this isn't about publicity."

"Who said anything about that? I'm talking about the trees. You ought to know what you've got." Papa sat in one of the office chairs and continued, "My great-grandfather bought this land when he came to America in 1880. We've been the only owners, the keepers of these trees for over one hundred years." He squared his shoulders.

"I know. You've mentioned this before," Mark said.

Maybe a thousand times.

"I taught this to your father. Greg understood the importance of what we do."

Mark slammed the desk drawer closed at the mention of his dad.

Brett spoke up. "I'm going to go work outside."

"Not yet—you can hear this too," Papa said. "Hans and Adeline started their life on this land. They cared for it through drought and flood and fire. One winter they lost two of their children."

Mark interjected, "I know, but they weren't selling trees."

"That's right—the Christmas tree market came later, but they laid the foundation. They made this land their treasure. Do you know what I mean by 'treasure'?" He looked at Mark with intensity. "Their hard work and sacrifice made it possible for their posterity, for *us*, to survive."

He's not going to start talking about my posterity, is he?

"Papa, I'm giving some money to the hospital, and I'm telling the manager at the apartments that we're donating trees for those families. That's all. I'm doing what my mom would have done," Mark said.

And I'm not saying anything about miracle trees.

"Your mom was a gem, that's for sure," Papa agreed. "She and your dad knew the trees."

There was that wistful look on Papa's face again. "Yeah, I miss them too." Mark said. *What did they know about the trees? Maybe if they were here they could explain Papa to me. Who am I kidding? If they were here, they wouldn't have to.*

"Brett, can you start selecting some trees we can send over there?" Mark asked.

Donna returned with some breakfast plates. "What are you asking Brett to do? I need his help in the craft barn today."

"And I had plans for him too," Papa said.

"I'm a popular guy." Brett smiled and accepted the food.

"I asked him to help with the trees we're donating while I go over to the hospital. But if you need him, Donna, he's all yours. I can go myself."

Mark didn't know what to expect when he walked to the information desk of the medical center. Usually when they donated money for the needs of a family, it was over the phone or through the mail, not in person.

The friendly volunteer gave him directions to the business office. Mark walked the stretch of two long hallways that formed an L around a courtyard. He met with an accounts manager who recognized his name from previous donations, and they had a brief conversation about the help Mark offered.

"Can you use the money for those who don't have insurance

first?" Mark asked. "And can this donation be anonymous? Is that possible?"

"I'm sure we can work that out," the manager replied.

As Mark left the office and neared the end of the first hallway, he saw a woman and her daughter coming out of the elevator.

"Hello." He stopped as his eyes met hers. "You're Angela?" Mark reached out and shook her hand.

"You're right," she said. "What are you doing here?"

"I had some business to take care of for the tree farm," he said.

"At the hospital?" her daughter asked.

Mark noticed the ID band on her wrist.

"Are you okay?" He looked to her and then to her mother.

"She's fine now," Angela answered as all three of them started walking slowly toward the lobby.

"There was a fire at our apartment, and I breathed in a lot of smoke," her daughter said.

"She wasn't in our apartment. We don't know what happened to our place," Angela tried to explain. "We're going there now to find out."

Scenes from the news flashed through Mark's mind.

"Oh, I am so sorry to hear that. That's why I'm here, or part of the reason I came—to help." *Didn't I just ask the accounts manager if I could remain anonymous?* "Anyway, we're donating trees to the families who need to find a new place to stay," he stammered. "I'll give you my number. I'll deliver a new tree to you, if you need one."

"Are we going to need to find another place to live, Mom?" her daughter interrupted.

"This is my daughter Caroline." Angela said to Mark. "We don't know yet." Angela responded to her daughter and shot Mark a questioning look. "That's generous of you. Not sure if we'll need *another* tree or not, but thank you."

Mark tried a different offer. "Well, you can come down to the farm anytime. On Saturdays, we have our 'hot dog, hot chocolate, and hay ride' event." He looked at her daughter, who had brightened at the suggestion. "I could even show you around."

"I'd love that!" Caroline said.

"I'm sure you would." Angela said. "Thanks for the invitation. We've got to go." She smiled half-heartedly at Mark and crossed the lobby to the exit.

Mark returned to the farm and found Donna and Brett in the office.

"This is so exciting—you have to come see this," Donna called to Mark. "Look at what Brett did for my blog."

"I fixed the website, like you asked me to do a month ago, and added a link to Donna's blog, the one she has for the crafts," Brett explained.

"And look at the clicks!"

"The hits. She means the hits to the website."

"And comments. I have twelve comments on yesterday's post!" she exclaimed.

"Is that a lot?" Mark knew better than to ask Donna a question like that.

"Of course it is. What's the matter with you? Before Channel 6 ran their story, no one knew my blog existed—except for my daughters and a few of my crafters. Look at this. Customers—real people—are reading it."

"You should take a look at some of these comments, Mark," Brett said. "One woman said her husband found a job a few days after they got a tree from us. And this woman didn't give her name, but she said a week after she bought a tree, her son called for the first time in a year." Brett scrolled down through the comments.

Mark stared at the screen. The news of the apartment fire did what Donna had said it would do—it took the place of any more stories about "miracle" trees. But what was this? Customers remembered. And believed. And miracles were happening?

"Do you see, Mark?" Donna asked. "Do you see all the good?"

He nodded reluctantly. "Wow, Donna, that's great. Thanks, Brett, for fixing the website."

Who's to say those things occurred because of a Shafer tree? Then again, who's to say they didn't?

CHAPTER 11

Angela and Caroline arrived at the apartments to find their building cordoned off with yellow caution tape, the blackened snow serving as an additional reminder of the fire. At least the smoke and clouds had left a clear afternoon sky. They parked and walked to the rental office. On their way, they saw the backside of the building where the fire started—the outer wall was missing and the edges, charred and exposed.

"It looks like a dollhouse," Caroline said.

"What do you mean?"

"I can see into the rooms and all the furniture, just like my dollhouse," she explained, "but without the black parts." She let go of her mother's hand and ran down the sidewalk.

"Wait, Caroline. Where are you going?" Angela called after her.

"To see our balcony. It doesn't look burned."

"That's good," Angela said, relieved. She followed Caroline to see for herself that at least the outside looked untouched by flames. "Let's go check in at the office."

A half-dozen people filled the small rental office and formed a scattered line in front of Mr. Buckley's desk. Angela couldn't see him through the crowd, but she did see Mrs. Shaw. They politely moved around a few people to greet her.

Mrs. Shaw threw her arms around Caroline. "Thank heavens you're all right. What a fright that was."

"Are you feeling okay? Did they keep you overnight too?" Angela asked.

"Yes, and I didn't sleep at all. We left the hospital at the same time this morning, but you didn't see me. Mark Shafer was talking to you, and I had to hurry."

"How do you know him?" Angela asked.

"He's a Shafer. Their family is almost Sutton itself. I know Donna better than Mark, though. I supply Christmas crafts to them, remember?"

"That's right."

"So sad about his parents," Mrs. Shaw said.

"What about them? Do you mean Donna?" Angela asked.

"No, Donna isn't his mother. Mark's parents died in a fire when he was a young boy. Donna was his mother's friend and she stayed, bless her, to help at the farm. She takes care of that family, too. They are salt-of-the-earth kind of people."

The kind of people who offer to deliver trees to sick children. The kind of people who deserve to be treated a little nicer than my cold shoulder.

"Are the two of you . . . are you seeing him?" Mrs. Shaw asked.

"Ah, no. He has a girlfriend. Not that it would matter if he didn't."

Every time he's seen me, I've looked pitiful.

Her mind cued the scenes like replays of crash-test-dummy videos—sitting in a truck that wouldn't start, trying to return the anonymous gift money—yeah, that was pleasant—and standing in the hospital hallway with her daughter after a sleepless night in a hospital chair.

"A man would be blind if he couldn't see your beauty, now wouldn't he?" Mrs. Shaw declared.

"Yes, he would," Mr. Buckley chimed in.

Angela hadn't noticed that the line had inched closer to his desk. She reddened and stepped behind Mrs. Shaw.

"Now, Don, I've talked to my daughter, and I'm changing my flight. I've got to get a few things from my apartment. The presents for my grandchildren were wrapped and ready, and I'm hoping they aren't ruined by the smoke. Even if the renter's insurance covers that kind of thing, I can't show up empty-handed." Mrs. Shaw handed Mr. Buckley a paper. "This is where I can be reached.

That's the area code for Portland. 503, Don, not 508—I've made that mistake before."

"Don't worry, I've got it," Mr. Buckley said.

Mrs. Shaw hugged Caroline and Angela again. "Now listen. I'm going to leave a little package outside my door before I leave today. Can you come by and pick it up?"

"Mrs. Shaw, you didn't have to do that."

"Sure I did—I'm leaving for the holiday. How else am I supposed to give you something for Christmas?"

Caroline clapped her hands.

"And block your ears, little one," she said to Caroline. "Angela, you'd best open it before the day—there are new stockings in the package. Caroline showed me the ones you've been using, and you needed some that were big enough to fit a decent-sized orange. And I put crackers in there—goodness, do you know what to do with those?" she asked hurriedly.

"You told me," Caroline piped up.

"Well, no surprises from me then." She laughed. "But do enjoy your holiday."

Mr. Buckley spoke up. "Angie. How've you been? I didn't come to the hospital—there's been so much to do here." Looking down to Caroline, he said, "I'm glad you're okay."

"I saw the yellow tape outside. It looks like our apartment is off limits. For how long?" Angela asked.

"Maybe a day or two. We'll find out from the fire department soon."

"Can we get some of our things, like Mrs. Shaw?" Angela didn't have presents to retrieve; she was just hoping for a change of clothes. "Do you have any idea how much smoke damage we had?"

"I don't, but yes, you can get what you need," Mr. Buckley said.

Angela noticed his disheveled hair and shirttail hanging out of his pants.

"Where will you be staying?" he asked.

There was an awkward silence as Angela looked at Caroline.

"I'm not sure right now."

"Didn't I tell you? We have a few vacant apartments in Building A. They're not furnished, of course, but they're available."

"For us? Really? Thank you. That's a relief."

"Unit 16 is a one-bedroom apartment like you have now. But

you might like unit 12. It's a two-bedroom ground level."

"That sounds nice. Is there an additional cost for the two-bedroom? Maybe we'd better stick with the smaller one."

"There's no cost. The owners have authorized me to use any vacant units we have as emergency housing for anyone with a damaged apartment. They even have some vacancies at a sister property if we fill up here."

The phone rang, and he turned his back on them as he answered it.

Caroline jumped up and down. "Does this mean I get my own room?" She started coughing. "I didn't even ask for that for Christmas."

"Maybe, but only for a few days," Angela answered. "We can't afford the rent for a two-bedroom."

Mr. Buckley finished and returned to Angela. "What were we doing? With the fire, the phones haven't stopped ringing. You know, Angie, I could use your help here now more than ever. What are your hours at the school? What do you say? Could you help me for a few hours next week?"

Angela heard what he said about the school and wondered exactly how long it would be before Caroline figured it out.

Please, for once, don't understand what he's saying.

"My mom doesn't have a job at the school yet," Caroline said.

Mr. Buckley raised his eyebrows.

"I've had my orientation, but I don't have a schedule yet," Angela blurted out.

Is that a lie?

"So come in on Monday," he said.

The crowded room, her daughter's admission—what could she say?

"Okay. We'll get settled this weekend, and I guess I'll be here Monday," she replied.

He gave Angela the key to unit 12 and they walked over to it. It was located in Building A, the building connected to the rental office.

How convenient, Mr. Buckley.

The apartment had more than an extra bedroom—the kitchen and the family room were both larger, and the ground-level patio had room for a table and chairs. Caroline ran from room to room and identified the master bedroom.

"Mom, you get a room with a bathroom all to yourself," she exclaimed.

"Don't run so much. You need to rest today."

Angela checked the kitchen for any odd smells in the fridge and microwave. The appliances were clean, and there was a combination of new carpet and fresh paint smell in the air.

"This is so great!" Caroline exclaimed.

How will she feel when we have to return to our tiny one-bedroom apartment in a few days?

"Come on—we've got work to do if we're going to sleep here tonight."

Angela parked the truck as close to the bottom of the stairwell as the caution tape would allow. She explained to Caroline that they were only bringing the things they most needed, as they would have to bring everything back. When they walked through the door, Angela braced herself for the worst.

"I can still smell smoke," Caroline said.

Angela exhaled and took another breath. "Yeah, I'm sure it will smell like this for a while."

"The fire didn't get this far. Everything's still here," she observed. "It just smells like a chimney."

Angela pulled a duffle bag and backpack from the closet, gave one to Caroline, and instructed her to pack enough clothes for the weekend. She checked her stack of mail for any bills that needed to be paid and grabbed a few bags and filled them with groceries she had bought the day before.

Was that just yesterday?

While they were walking out the door, Caroline stopped and looked at the Christmas tree.

"Can we come back for this?" she asked.

"The tree? Oh, Caroline, I don't think so. We're not going to haul it down the stairs and across the courtyard for two or three days. It's already decorated." Was this the start of a new battle?

"Can we ask Mr. Shafer for a tree for our new apartment?" Caroline asked.

Reminded of the conversation with Mark, Angela felt a twinge of guilt. She had no plans to call and ask for a tree for an apartment they would only be in for a couple of days, but she wished she'd been more gracious when he offered.

"Sweetheart, we don't have a 'new' apartment. We're staying in a temporary one. We're coming back in a few days."

Caroline looked crushed.

"Can we bring something for Christmas?"

"Like what?"

"Can I bring your nativity set?" she asked as she looked at it longingly.

Angela set the grocery bags down in front of the door. She picked up the case and began putting the pieces into their corresponding velvet compartments. Caroline helped. The place for the lamb remained empty.

"I'm sorry I lost the lamb," Caroline said.

"It's okay," Angela insisted. "Don't worry about it."

"Will we ever find it?"

"Maybe," she said. *Probably not.*

"What did Florinda tell you about the wise men?" Caroline asked.

Angela sighed. Her daughter's energy seemed to increase as Angela's waned.

"The wise men? 'Don't give up your search for Jesus,' I think she said."

"What does that mean?"

"The wise men travelled a great distance. It must have been a long journey, but they didn't stop until they found Jesus as a child." Angela almost closed the case, but Caroline reached for another piece.

"What about him? What did she say about Joseph?"

Too worn out to resist her daughter's earnest inquiry, Angela explained, "Florinda said, 'when you find someone as loving and as loyal as Joseph, keep him close to your heart.' "

Caroline reached for the figure and tilted her head. "You haven't found someone like that yet, have you?" she asked.

Angela took the figure back, put it in the case and closed it. She spoke the obvious answer hanging in the air.

"No. I haven't."

CHAPTER 12

One week since Mark accepted John Jackson's offer, and one week since he bought the ring. The media attention had subsided, just as Donna said it would. He and John settled on the details of the sale. Five acres. Mark had saved five acres of the land that Papa's cabin and the craft barn were on. The tentative close date was early February—a relatively short time considering the size of the farm, yet too long to keep the sale a secret from Papa. And much too long for Mark to carry Natalie's ring around in his coat pocket.

Maybe an engagement would be a good diversion.

The last thing he needed to secure financing for the home on Hickory Street was some of the money John Jackson had promised him for his "help" with the sale. If he could have half of what John had promised, he could have things in place before Christmas.

He called Dave on his way to pick up flowers for Natalie. "Hey, I've got a question for you," Mark said as he drove.

"Does it have to do with putting in an offer?"

"I'm still waiting on that one. It should be soon, though." Mark didn't wait to hear Dave's impatient answer. "So I was wondering. Could we go see the house again, with Natalie? I really want her to see it."

"And you probably want to go tonight, right?" Dave asked.

"Is that okay? Do you have plans? We're kind of celebrating something." Mark didn't explain further.

Dave sighed into the phone. "How about five o'clock?"

"Great. One more thing. When we're done looking at it, could you, I don't know, leave us alone for a few minutes?"

"Yeah, sure—wait. How many minutes?"

"Five or maybe ten? I'm asking her to marry me." Mark's stomach tightened in anticipation as he said it out loud.

"Whoa, Mark. You're proposing? At a house you don't own yet? And you only need five or ten minutes? I'm not an expert, but when I proposed to Crystal, I took her out for half the day. We went down to the Gorge, one of her favorite places. And then we came back to town and I proposed at the Gazebo. It was the Fourth of July. I timed it right before the fireworks," Dave bragged.

"I remember you telling me about that."

Actually, I remember you telling everyone about that.

"I can't leave you there for an hour." Dave said.

Mark clenched his jaw. He pulled into the parking lot of the flower shop.

"I guess I'm not as cool as you are—but Natalie is excited about the music studio. I think she'll think it's romantic. How about fifteen minutes?"

Dave was silent.

"For old time's sake?"

"Okay, Mark. Fifteen minutes. It's not like I could lose my license or anything. If I did, I'd need my old job pruning trees at your farm." Dave laughed. Mark thanked him and ended the call.

He stared at the varied arrangements of flowers. He had an unexpected memory of the sunflower bag from the picture of his mom. He looked around, but certainly didn't see any sunflower bouquets. He finally asked for a dozen red roses.

She wouldn't understand the sunflowers anyway.

Back at the farm, Mark entered the side door of the farmhouse and walked through the dining room to hide the flowers in the kitchen. Not before Papa saw him and followed him inside.

"A man only has a few reasons to carry a bouquet of roses like that." He said.

"Hi Papa, I'm setting these down and coming right out."

"Either he's done something wrong . . . or he's about to do something right." Papa smiled. "Which is it?"

"Couldn't it be a special occasion, like a birthday?" Mark asked.

"It could. So is it Natalie's birthday?"

Mark set the flowers in a vase he found and sighed. *Well, here goes.*

"No, I'm asking Natalie to marry me tonight."

"Well I'd say it's 'bout time."

"She still needs to say yes," Mark added.

"Why wouldn't she?" Papa finished a drink of water, set the glass down and walked towards the door. "Good idea, proposing now. If she likes, she can spend time here at the farm this Christmas. She'll get a good idea of the life she has waiting for her."

Mark clanged the vase against the side of the counter. At least it wasn't a question and he could pretend to focus on the flowers. "I'll be out in a few minutes." He said.

He did his best to help with customers for a few hours, but he kept rehearsing the proposal in his mind. He left the sales lot and found Brett loading a tree onto one of the farm trucks.

"What are you doing there?" Mark asked.

"We got a call from Mr. Buckley at the Blackstone Apartments. He asked if we still had a tree for one of their residents, one who had to relocate after the fire."

"Great—I'm glad he called us." Mark walked over and helped him secure the tree. "I'll deliver this one."

"Are you sure?" Brett asked. "I don't mind doing it."

Mark looked at his watch. He had several more hours before he could pick up Natalie.

"Thanks, but I've got it."

Anything to help pass the time.

CHAPTER 13

The fire department gave the clearance for residents to move back into the apartments not damaged by the fire. For a week, Mr. Buckley had encouraged Angela to stay in the larger, temporary apartment. He had valid reasons—there weren't any prospective tenants interested in it, and the management company had approved the "emergency housing" stay for the entire month. However, she knew Mr. Buckley had at least one more reason—she was much closer to the office.

Living out of a backpack and sleeping on the floor was getting old for Angela, but Caroline loved her own room. Angela told her they would stay for a few more days and then move back.

"How about until the last day of school before Christmas break," Caroline bargained.

"That's a week and half away!" Angela noticed her daughter's face and softened. "We'll see."

As for the rental office, she couldn't complain about the convenience of the location or the hours. The "commute" consisted of a short walk, less than a block from her temporary apartment, and she could work during the time Caroline was at school. She only had to ignore one irritation.

"How are ya today, Angie?" Mr. Buckley asked when she arrived.

"Fine and you?" She managed to sound civil, though cheerful was a stretch.

Should I ask him to call me Angela?

"If you have a minute, I need to run something by you," he said.

He's in a good mood. Maybe he won't be offended.

"Sure. What's up?"

"You're doing a great job here. I can't tell you how nice it has been this week, having your help with things." He rocked back in his desk chair. "You've learned the software better than me."

That's not hard to do.

"Anyway, Angie, I thought I'd check—"

She'd reached her limit. "I haven't mentioned this before, but I prefer 'Angela'," she said as casually as she could.

"I—I didn't realize."

He looked a little wounded.

"My ex-husband used to call me 'Angie,' so I'd rather be called something else."

"Say no more. 'Angela' it is. While we're at it, you can call me 'Don'." He brightened. "No more Mr. Buckley around here."

Terrific.

"So, like I was saying, I checked with our management company, and I worked out a deal for you. If you continue to work at least twenty hours a week, you can stay in unit 12 for a reduced rate." He tapped his pen on the desk and looked expectantly at Angela.

"What kind of a reduced rate?"

I don't remember asking you to work out a deal for me.

"That's the best part. It turns out to be a hundred dollars less than what you're paying in the one-bedroom. That's a steal!"

"Yeah, that sounds good, but about the 'twenty hours' requirement," she began. "Christmas break starts next week. Once Caroline is out of school, I won't have a sitter. Mrs. Shaw won't be back until January. I'm not in a position to commit to that many hours."

"We can fudge it. I mean I'll take care of it, and you can move the rest of your stuff this weekend." He beamed.

Fudge?

"Mr. Buckley, I don't feel right—"

"Don—call me Don. Yes, it's a lot to take in. Believe me, I was surprised myself. They usually offer reduced rates to full-time employees, but with all you've been through, they agreed. And let's keep this quiet. I've had a few other residents ask about the assistant manager position."

"Uh, I don't know what to say," she said

How do I get in to these predicaments? Of course I'd like to live in a larger apartment for less money. But why does that have to include working for 'Don'?

"The school is supposed to call me back anytime. I don't know what my schedule will be."

"Even if you have to work evenings, that's fine. Don't worry about the hours. I said I'll take care of that." He stood and put on his coat. "I've got to check on unit 43—Walter parked his car in front of the dumpsters again. I'm going to have to buy cones or something."

Angela settled in at her makeshift desk.

"One more thing. I know Caroline has been begging you to move your tree. I called the Shafer Farm. You knew they had donated trees, right? They'll be delivering one to your new apartment later this afternoon." He flashed a proud grin and walked out the door.

Angela fumed to herself. Who did he think he was? Caroline would be happy, but he had no right to make that call for her. She allowed the work of processing two rental applications to take her mind off things. She had a couple of hours before she left to pick up Caroline from school.

A tenant came in and asked for Mr. Buckley. He hadn't returned so Angela offered to help the tenant if she could. The resident explained that she needed to renew her lease.

Angela found the file that contained renewal contracts. Mr. Buckley hadn't trained her on these, but she'd learned the new tenant lease and this looked much simpler. There was already a pre-filled contract with the woman's name on it in the file. It didn't take more than ten minutes to finish, and when they were done, Angela was alone in the office again. She looked for the place to put the completed contract.

She flipped through a folder with more unsigned renewal contracts. A few had "rewrite for accuracy" scrawled across the top. She scanned over the printed pages, obviously sent from the home office, which looked more accurate than Mr. Buckley's handwritten ones. She found the "original" lease of the one she had just completed.

That's unusual.

There it was in the middle of the page, the first month's discount for renewing—gone. And in its place was the regular rental rate.

What is he doing?

Angela scoured the pages, looking for an explanation. She looked at other leases and found the same pattern. The home office sent contracts that contained a discount, and he removed it. It didn't add up—literally. She checked some of the recent deposit logs and had a sinking feeling. He was charging residents a higher rate than what the home office expected. She couldn't figure out how he was putting the extra money in his own pocket, but something was wrong. She heard a noise and shoved the file closed. She was late to pick up Caroline. She returned the file to the drawer and grabbed her coat.

Mr. Buckley stomped his way in the door, snow flying off his boots.

"Just enough snow to make it messy out there," he said with a silly grin.

"I've got to run and get Caroline," she said, avoiding eye contact.

Angela picked up Caroline from school and half listened to her day while mulling over what had happened at the office. Would her discovery have any impact on what she had agreed to earlier that morning? It was another impossible situation. She hadn't asked for this assistant manager job or for any special favors from Mr. Buckley. And the last thing she wanted was to be a part of his dishonesty.

Maybe I'm jumping to conclusions. There could be an explanation for what he's doing. If the school calls with my schedule, I'll quit the office job and figure out how to pay the higher rent.

"Who's at our apartment, Mom?" Caroline asked as they got out of the truck and rounded the corner to their place.

In her preoccupation with Mr. Buckley, Angela had forgotten all about the tree.

"Is that Mr. Shafer with another tree?" Caroline asked, running toward him.

"Wait!" She quickened her step.

Angela took a deep breath and walked up to the door. There he was, waiting with that warm smile, like he had in the hospital hallway. Mrs. Shaw was always right, wasn't she?

"I didn't know Mr. Buckley had called you," she said. "We could have moved our other tree. This was nice of you, though. Aren't you busy just weeks before Christmas?"

"I'm glad to do it. I hope you like this one," he said, smiling at Caroline.

Angela opened the door and watched Mark carry the tree inside. *He makes it look so easy.*

He leaned the tree against the corner of the wall in the living room.

"Thank you, thank you!" Caroline said. "I love it."

Mark glanced around the empty room.

"It's not all we need," Angela said, wanting to explain. "But we're moving the rest of our furniture this weekend."

"I see. Did you lose a lot in the fire?"

"No, our apartment had some smoke damage, but not much. This was a temporary apartment until today."

"My mom is going to be the assistant manager for Mr. Buckley," Caroline offered in her usual "say-more-than-her-mom-wants" fashion.

Angela stammered to clarify, "It's just part-time, but this unit is closer to the office."

"And it's bigger. I get my own room. Come see it!"

"I'm sure Mr. Shafer needs to get back to the tree farm, Caroline," Angela said as she walked over and opened the door. "Thank you again for the tree." She motioned to it and felt the heat rise in her cheeks.

He looked again at Caroline. "Are you feeling better?"

"Lots," she said.

"We're having hayrides at the farm tomorrow, and my offer is still good for that tour," Mark said.

"Can we, Mom? Can we?" Caroline asked.

"I'm not sure when we'll have time." Angela paused. "Maybe next year."

Maybe our life will be less complicated then.

"No. Don't wait that long," he said rather gravely. "I have an idea. How about dinner? Would you and your family like to join us on Christmas Day? We have a big meal, and we always like to invite new . . . new friends."

"Can my grandma come? She's mostly the only family we have, sort of."

If Angela had followed her instincts, she would have flatly declined his offer. No, they didn't need to have dinner at the farm, and what did he mean by "new friends" anyway? She wasn't in the mood to sit at a table with him and his girlfriend. And what was Caroline doing inviting her grandmother?

Like that would ever happen.

"That would be great, yes. Bring her. I'd love to meet her." Mark smiled.

Why does he have to be so genuine?

Angela opened her mouth to answer, and somewhere between looking at Caroline's pleading face, the fresh-cut pine tree, and Mark's eager eyes, her instinct and reason lost the majority vote.

"Sure. That's very generous of you. I'll have to ask my mother." She smiled back at Mark and shot Caroline a look. "But we'll come."

"Great! I'll tell Donna to plan for three more, just in case." He winked at Caroline. "We'll eat around noon."

As soon as Angela closed the door, Caroline squealed and threw her arms around her mom's waist. "Do you know what this means?"

"Yes. I'm a glutton for punishment."

"No, whatever that is. It means we get to have a big family dinner for Christmas, like I wanted," she declared. "Let's go move our stuff!"

CHAPTER 14

Mark left the Blackstone Apartments and checked his watch to make sure he'd have enough time to drive back to the farm and get his BMW and then pick up Natalie. He took the turnpike, and as he drove, he planned the proposal. At least, he tried, but it seemed his thoughts had a mind of their own and wanted to sort out this Angela. He didn't know she was the resident in unit 12 that Brett had told him about. She had been quick to mention that Mr. Buckley called for the tree, but she did let him in and she had thanked him. She had even smiled at him.

So?

The empty apartment had given him no more clues about her.

How long has she been single? Does she have a boyfriend? She must. Why does that matter to me? What am I doing? And what will Natalie say when she finds out I invited Angela to Christmas dinner?

He reached to put in a different music CD, but this was his work truck and not his BMW. No CD player here.

I'll have to explain that it's part of our farm tradition—we have neighbors and friends share Christmas dinner with us every year. What can she say to that?

He dropped off the truck, picked up his car and flowers, and raced to where Natalie worked. He arrived a few minutes before five and waited outside her store to surprise her. Temperatures had dropped ten degrees overnight and it hadn't even reached twenty degrees all day. She walked out with a co-worker.

He approached them on the sidewalk before they crossed the parking lot to their cars. Her friend pointed to him, and Natalie turned and froze. He quickened his step, excited by the look of surprise on both their faces. She turned to her friend, said something, and turned back. Her friend took off speed-walking across the parking lot.

"What are you doing here?" Natalie asked.

"Happy Friday!" Mark said. "I came to pick you up so we could ride together. It's out of the way, but I'll bring you back after dinner. There's something I want you to see."

He handed her the bouquet. She hesitated before she took it.

"You're not allergic to roses, are you?"

"Yeah—I mean, no. They're beautiful. Sorry, I'm just *shocked* to see you here." She looked over her shoulder in the direction of her friend.

"I didn't embarrass you, did I?" Mark started to doubt his attempt to be more romantic, or whatever Dave was.

"No, I told Erin I'd call her later."

"Good. Let's go, then."

The sun had set and the roads were slick. Natalie asked Mark about the sale of the farm and how it was coming along. He told her about the tentative close date for February.

"So this will be the last Christmas that the Shafer tree farm will be open?" she asked.

Did she have to state the obvious? "Yes, I guess so. Unless Papa and Donna decide to continue operating the craft barn. You wouldn't believe how much her business has picked up in the last few weeks." His stomach tightened again. He still hadn't told Donna about the sale.

"And you're sure your grandfather doesn't know what you're doing? What will he do if he finds out? Would he try to stop you?" she probed.

"I hope not. What can he do now that I own the farm? Don't worry," he said. But he did worry. Even as he tried to reassure her, he felt the doubt press upon his plans. *What will this really mean for Papa? Am I doing the right thing?*

"At this point, you're so close, I'd hate to see anything get in the way of your dream." She said as she smiled.

They arrived at the house, and Dave was on the porch waiting.

"Come on in, you two. You picked the coldest night in December to be here."

Mark and Natalie walked from room to room. He showed off the studio in the basement, and they returned to Dave in the kitchen.

"What do you think?" Dave asked.

Mark waited to hear what Natalie had to say. She looked back and forth between the two of them.

"Oh, what do I think? It's a nice place. A great space with *four* bedrooms. Wow!" She looked at Mark. "It fits you," she offered sweetly.

"Hey, I've got a call. I'll take it outside in my car." Dave nodded to Mark.

He took the cue. "Natalie, I forgot to show you something downstairs in the studio."

They walked back down to the finished basement and he opened the door to the studio. He pulled out one of the cushioned stools and motioned for her to sit. He glanced at his watch. Could he do this before Dave returned?

He slipped off his gloves and his coat and pulled out the ring box.

"You're wearing a suit!"

"I told you we were celebrating, didn't I?"

"Yes, but what?" she stopped.

He inadvertently glanced at his watch again, opened the box, and asked, "Natalie, will you marry me?"

She stood up, her mouth falling open. "Mark, are you serious? We haven't talked about this." She looked at him and back at the ring. "I didn't expect this. One minute, you're showing me this house—"

"Wait, I was going to kneel. Should I kneel?" This wasn't going at all like he'd planned.

"No, you don't have to kneel."

He knelt anyway. "After I met you, I felt like my dreams became possible. You've understood my passion for music and you've supported the steps I've taken to make that dream become a reality. I want you to be a part of that future with me," he said, gaining confidence as he finished.

Natalie sat back down and stared at the ring. This was the moment where he planned she'd say "yes" or some version of it, and maybe be excited. He took the ring from the box and held her hand.

"May I?"

She nodded.

"There. I love you, Natalie."

"I guess you do. I love you too."

They hugged, and Mark started to kiss her.

"Are you down there, Mark?" Dave called from the top of the stairs.

That could not have been fifteen minutes.

"Let's go to dinner," Mark said. He grabbed his coat and took her by the hand.

As they left the house Mark thanked Dave. "I owe you one."

They finished dinner, and Mark took Natalie back to the store where her car was parked. He felt like he carried the conversation most of the night—Natalie was quieter than usual. The few times she did talk, she asked questions about his family.

"Did you say you have a sister in LA?" she asked.

"I do. She usually calls around this time of year to say she isn't coming to visit for Christmas. Who knows, maybe this year she'll come. Do you want to meet her? She's very artsy, and very southern Californian."

"You're not that close, then. Does she know about me?"

Mark was confused at first, and then it clicked.

"Not yet, but don't worry. I love you, and my family will too," he said.

"I doubt it," she muttered.

Yeah, it may take Papa and Donna a while before they love her like I do.

He leaned across to her seat and kissed her good night. "I'll call you tomorrow."

Engaged. Where was the relief he expected to feel? Or at least the excitement? Instead, Natalie seemed shocked, and rightly concerned about the family.

Maybe we should wait a few days before we say anything.

CHAPTER 15

M r. Buckley had asked Angela to come in on Saturday. She only agreed because Caroline was able to play with a friend from school. She could put in some extra hours so he wouldn't mind if she took a few days off around the holiday. Maybe the phones and office traffic would be light.

"Good morning, Angela." His voice was cooler.

"Hi Mr. Buck—uh, Don. How are you today?"

"I'm fine, sort of."

Okay, then. That cafeteria job looks better all the time.

"Hey, did you help Mrs. Carlson with her lease renewal yesterday?" he asked with the same cool tone.

"I did. She came in right before I left. You weren't here, so—"

"Where did you put it?"

Oh, no. Did I put it in the wrong place?

Angela walked over to his file cabinet, cringing. She avoided getting any closer to where he worked than she had to. "I put it right back in this file." Her voice wavered as she answered. When she opened the folder and flipped through the contracts, it wasn't there. "Unless I forgot to file it . . ."

"Did you put it in this folder, by chance?" He sat in his chair with the home office folder in his hand and held it up for her to see. Angela put the other file away slowly.

"I don't know. Did I?"

"Well, would you look at that? Here it is," he said dryly.

What's with him?

"I was thinking, *Angela*, that if you are going to be working here at least twenty hours a week, we should have a little talk about our office procedures." He closed the folder and pushed his chair back from the desk. "You're pretty quick, the way you pick up on things. I should have known. I mean, if I'd known how *helpful* you were going to be, I would have been more specific."

Angela walked over to her desk and pretended to be interested in the paperwork on it.

"I'll take care of the lease renewals and the maintenance calls. You're here to handle the phones and the filing and a few other things during our first-of-the-month crunch."

He spoke with a scolding tone she hadn't heard from him before. And she didn't like it.

"That's fine." She swallowed some of her pride and continued, "Sorry if I filed that lease in the wrong place. I won't do that again."

"Mistakes happen. Let me just say this—we're in this together. You keep my secrets, and I'll keep yours."

What?

"I don't have any secrets. What are you talking about?" she asked, dumbfounded. She stopped shuffling papers and glared at him. The office felt small; couldn't someone walk in and need something?

"Don't play dumb now. It's too late for that. If you keep to yourself, I won't mention our deal to home office, all right?"

"What deal? Look, Mr. Buckley, I don't know what you're talking about, but I never asked for any special treatment. There's been some misunderstanding. I won't do any more lease renewals, okay?" Angela's heart pounded, her palms wet.

"Simmer down now. I didn't mean to ruffle your feathers." He continued, "We're still going to get along fine. Do the work I ask you to do, and you and your daughter can keep a roof over your heads."

Was that a threat? Her stomach twisted into knots. She fumbled for her coat. "I've got to go pick up Caroline," she said.

She didn't wait for him to ask if she was coming back later. She left the office and took deep breaths of the chilled air as fast as she could to ease the swelling nausea. She muttered things under her breath, things like "how dare he?" and "who does he think he is?" And a few other words like "obnoxious" and "cheat" while she was at it.

When Angela picked up her daughter, all Caroline talked about were hot dogs, hot chocolate, and hayrides.

"Please, Mom, please let's go. We can unpack later."

Angela checked the gauge on her dash and hoped they'd have enough gas to make it there and back. "I think that's a great idea, Caroline."

At least I can put Mr. Buckley and that office behind me.

The sun shone bright in a clear, cloudless sky, and it had warmed up to fifty degrees. They passed the dairy farm, and Caroline said something about the cows.

"Did you hear me? I wonder what it's like to milk a cow," she said.

"I couldn't say. We didn't have any of those in the Elliott home." Angela looked across the snow-covered pasture and off to the ridge of trees behind it. "We didn't have views like that, either."

They took the right turn after the Shafer Tree Farm sign.

"I like this part of the trip," Caroline said.

"Why is that?"

"This road looks so cool, with all the trees on both sides," she said. "It feels like we're in the middle of the forest. Doesn't it feel enchanted?"

Angela glanced at her daughter's raised-eyebrow expression. She looked into the dense wood as far as the sunlight allowed and shook her head.

"Look at the trees. It's like they're guards." Caroline continued.

"Guarding what?" Angela asked.

"I don't know. Secrets?"

"What an imagination you have."

The farm buzzed with families. Caroline and Angela walked over to the tent set up next to the craft barn where they were serving hot chocolate and hot dogs. They ate at a picnic table, and Caroline recognized a girl from her school class. Angela visited with her mother for a few minutes until Caroline asked to see the craft tables.

They browsed the specialty decorations—everything from

gorgeous handmade Christmas quilts to alphabet blocks that spelled NOEL. Angela looked up from a table of ornaments and saw Mark Shafer walking through the maze of customers. She turned her attention back to the crafts and hoped she'd go unnoticed.

No such luck. He approached the table where they stood. "Glad you made it today," he said to Angela. "Looks like another hayride is about to start." He pointed the wagon out to Caroline. "Papa's driving this one. You'll get an extra-long ride."

Caroline looked at her mom with pleading eyes.

"Yes, go ahead. See if your friend wants to go too," Angela said, and watched Caroline run off so she wouldn't miss the ride.

She looked back at Mark; another customer had stopped him. He was answering the woman's question with his full attention. She tried not to stare, but it was easy to see why Mrs. Shaw spoke so highly of him.

She gradually walked away from them as the customer continued to engage him in conversation.

"Angela," he called.

Surprised, she turned around. He was following her.

"I owe you that tour. I can't show you as much as Papa can with his hayride, but if you're interested, we could take a walk," he said.

Did he just say we could take a walk? The answer is yes. YES. Okay, don't look so obvious.

"Are you sure you aren't needed here?" She nodded at the customers milling around.

"They can manage without me for a few minutes," he said as he flashed a good-natured smile. "Here, this way."

They walked side by side between the craft barn and the farmhouse on a path that took them beyond Papa's cabin to the back lot of trees. He described how their business had grown over the last ten years, and how they had tried to build and plant to keep up with it.

This was different than the first night she came to the farm. She was less annoyed, yes, but she could see Mark better, not because of the daylight. He opened up about the farm. He explained all the work he and his family put into the trees. She didn't think of Papa as a pushy salesman anymore. This was their life.

"Look, I'm sorry about accusing you of giving money to me for publicity. I jumped to conclusions," she admitted.

"Don't mention it. I've been accused of worse things." He laughed. "I wish I knew who gave it to you, though, and how the news picked it up. That created a stir around here."

"Wasn't that good for business?"

"In one way." He looked off above the tree line. "But we didn't need the story about the miracles trees getting out of hand. It doesn't help business if we're the laughing stock of Sutton."

"You couldn't be that. You and your family are loved by so many." *Like Mrs. Shaw, for one.* "So what is it with the trees? *Do* they cause miracles?" she asked, checking his face for clues.

"My grandfather says they do."

"Do you see them differently than your grandfather does?"

"That's a good way to put it. He certainly has his own way of seeing things." He stopped at a tree, reached out, and held one of the boughs. "He's been the keeper of these trees, or grown them, his whole life. I don't know what he knows." Mark glanced at Angela.

"So *are* they miracle trees?" she asked, more interested now that he wasn't giving her a straight answer.

He reddened. "They could be. Papa's convinced there are 'believers,' and they are the ones who get the miracles. Who am I to say they don't?"

"They are the ones who can *see* the miracles? Is that what he means?"

"Maybe." Mark shrugged and changed the subject. "What did you do with the money? Didn't you need it to pay rent?"

"Yes, I paid it." She paused. "And then we had the fire. Thanks again for bringing another tree. And inviting us today—this has been fun for Caroline."

"And what has it been for you?" He looked at her and back at the trees.

"Me? I'm fine. I mean, yeah, this is great."

This would be a good place to say something nice.

"I hadn't noticed until now how peaceful this place can be, at least out here. It's quiet and serene. I think it's having a calming effect on me," she admitted. Was it the farm or Mark, though? She couldn't tell.

She continued, "Do you love working with the land? How fun was it growing up here?" She ended her sentence abruptly, as she remembered what Mrs. Shaw had said.

Mark stopped and looked directly at her. He didn't say anything for a minute. He pivoted and looked behind her at the back of the farmhouse. "You've heard about the fire we had here?"

"I'm sorry. I should stop talking."

"It's fine—most people know. And to answer your question, yes, I loved growing up here, but it changed when my parents died. I've tried, but it's hard to love it the same way they did." Mark didn't turn back around and resume the direction they had been walking. Instead, he took slow steps back the way they came. Angela turned around too.

Way to mess up the moment.

"I can understand. Is there anything else you love?" she asked.

Mark was less talkative and continued to look ahead to the crowds at the sales lot.

"Yeah, music. I plan to go into music production."

Another musician?

"Would you leave the farm?" *Was that too personal?*

He didn't answer. "What about you? Do you want to work somewhere else besides the apartments?"

"Um, I didn't mean—yes, I do. I don't plan to stay at the apartments. I studied music before . . ."

Before I got married and then divorced.

He looked at her with a question on his face.

"I'd work here over the apartments in a heartbeat," she said.

Mark didn't respond and looked like he was focused on something up ahead.

Now it sounds like I'm asking for a job. What is the matter with me?

Angela noticed the hayride coming to an end and quickened her step to get there.

They arrived in time to greet the children. Caroline asked if she could go on the next ride and if Angela could ride too.

"Another one? We need to go, Caroline."

Angela turned to thank Mark for the tour. Before she could speak, another woman approached them. She stood close to Mark. Very close. Her hands were deep in her pockets, but she leaned into him with her shoulder, all while staring at Angela.

"Natalie, I'd like you to meet, uh, this is Angela," he stammered. "Angela, this is my . . . Natalie."

"Wait, Angela from the news story—Mark you didn't tell me we had a celebrity at the farm today." Natalie trained her eyes on Mark as she spoke the disingenuous words.

"We're going now." Angela said and nodded at Caroline. "We have boxes to unpack at home. It was nice to meet you." She said to Natalie.

If nice can mean awkward or awful, then yes, nice to meet you.

"Hey, I'm glad you came to the farm today. I hope you enjoyed the ride," Mark said, but his tone was different and he focused his attention more on Caroline.

"Thanks." Angela tried using her disinterested face, but she wasn't sure if it worked.

"So do we still get to come back for Christmas dinner?" The question burst from Caroline like a jack-in-the-box.

"Yes, that's right, Christmas dinner. We'd love to have you." Mark's arm went around his girlfriend's shoulders.

"Oh, I'm not sure—" Angela said.

"She's going to call my grandma soon. I'm sure she'll say yes because we haven't spent Christmas together for years."

Thanks, Caroline! Let's get out of here.

"Great. Hope she makes it too," Mark said.

CHAPTER 16

The ten days or so before the holiday were the busiest days of the season. There wouldn't be any let-up in the flow of customers until they closed the farm on Christmas Eve. Donna cooked a big dinner for the "farm family" on Christmas, a tradition that had gone unbroken for decades. Where she found the energy, Mark didn't know. It was Monday morning, and he was ready for a vacation.

After breakfast, he helped Papa plow the snow out of the parking lot. His cell phone rang as he was finishing the last section.

"Hi Mark, this is Dave."

"I'm glad you called," Mark said, but Dave continued talking.

"I just got a courtesy call from the agent for the house on Hickory. She said they've got an offer. It sounds like an investor, probably out-of-state."

"Okay, so what does that mean? We need to beat their price?"

"It's a cash offer, Mark, for a little less than what they're asking. For as long as this house has sat empty, the sellers are more than ready."

"What are you saying?" Mark asked.

"I'm saying that unless you can come up with the asking price *in cash*, there isn't anything I can do for you."

"But I should have the money for my down payment any day. I can offer more than the asking price." He panicked. "I'll call my lender right now."

"Mark, do you hear me? It's a cash offer. I can't work a miracle."

Miracle. He would have to use that word.

"I get it—I understand. Thanks. I need to go." Mark said.

"I'm happy to look for some other houses. You could look into what it would cost to convert a bedroom into a studio. That might be a better way to go," he said.

Mark ended the call and jumped out of the small plow truck.

"Hey, where are you going in such a hurry?" Papa asked.

"For a walk."

"We're here to talk to Mark Shafer." Two men stood behind the counter in the front room of the farmhouse. One had a weather-worn face and wore a heavy coat. The other man wore a collared shirt under his sport jacket and held a clipboard.

"That's me. What can I do for you gentlemen?" Mark asked.

They don't look like reporters. That's good.

"We're from Marshall Brothers, and we're here for the property inspection," the man said and handed over a business card.

Mark nervously checked the room to make sure no one heard them. He tapped the counter with the business card and put it down, out of his hands.

"I wasn't notified you'd be coming today," he said. "This is our busiest time, in about two weeks it will be much quieter here."

And I can make sure we won't have company.

"The crowd won't interfere with what we need to do," the man explained with a resolute tone in his voice. "This is the inspection for the lender. The survey for title insurance takes much longer."

"Right," Mark said. "If I had gotten a call, I could have been ready. I can accommodate you any day next week."

The man looked down at the paper on his metal clipboard case.

Mark glanced over his shoulder. He didn't act quickly enough. Donna and Brett walked in from outside. He had less than thirty seconds to escort the men out of the farmhouse with as little commotion as possible.

"Great. Follow me," he said loudly. The men's faces displayed surprise. "I'm happy to help you with as many trees as you'd like," he said. "Brett, can you watch the register?"

Mark motioned to a side door behind the counter and said thanks to Brett. He saw the interest on Donna's face.

"I'll help you in the barn tonight, Donna," Mark said.

The men walked to the door and Mark caught up with them. He ushered them out before they could say anything else.

Once they were all outside, Mark announced, "Let me show you where the cabin is—the part of the land you need to see is behind it. There's a private road."

"You're not required to stay with us, if that's a problem," the man with the clipboard explained.

"Thanks, that might be best," Mark said as he walked them around to the parking lot. "And can you do me a favor? If you happen to meet my grandfather—he wears a green coat and red pin with our farm name on it—can you—"

"You mean him?" The shorter man asked, pointing.

Mark turned to see Papa approaching.

The man continued, "What? Do you need us to pretend to be customers or something?"

"Could you?" Mark asked.

"If it's going to be that much of a problem, we can reschedule." The man with the clipboard didn't hide his annoyance.

"Mark, are these good men leaving here without a tree?" Papa asked. He reached out and shook their hands. "Call me Papa Shafer. Is my grandson taking care of you?"

"So far," the shorter man said cautiously.

"Did you find what you're looking for?"

"Not yet." The other gentleman looked at Mark.

"Papa, they stopped in to see what we offered. They weren't prepared to haul a tree. They're coming back," Mark said, nodding to the parking lot exit.

"Sounds good. Don't wait too long," Papa warned. "Christmas will come and go before you know it."

The men walked off to their truck, while Mark engaged Papa in some conversation as a distraction. They strolled around the farmhouse and back in through the side door. Mark was coming down from the adrenaline rush of the previous ten minutes when he saw Brett and Donna at the counter.

"Thanks again, Brett." Mark noticed a few customers standing by the fireplace and one looking at the postcard wall.

"What's this?" Donna looked at Mark and held up the business card.

"Whatcha got there?" Papa chimed in.

"What are land surveyors doing here?" she asked defiantly.

"They were looking for a Christmas tree," Papa replied, looking to Mark for confirmation.

The next few moments unfolded in slow motion for Mark. He met Donna's eyes and then Papa's. He could see the recognition, starting like an avalanche, and there was nothing he could do to keep the mountain from falling on top of him.

Papa shook his head and muttered. "It's just as I thought."

"What are you talking about?" Mark asked.

"These trees can survive drought, disease, and a thousand floods." He paused and continued quietly, "but nothing can save them from fools."

Mark opened his mouth, but he had no words, no reply. Not that it mattered. Papa had already turned his back and was heading out the door. Brett didn't look up from the cash register where customers were beginning to form a line.

Donna, however, did not hold back. "What are you thinking?" She waved her arms up in exasperation. "You want them to bulldoze the farm and what? Name the streets after the trees? Spruce Ave or Pine Lane? What about Shafer Way? Where will that street lead?"

In desperation, Mark pointed out that there were customers present.

"Don't tell me about the customers." She started. "Do you really care about them? Or your family? Or anyone but yourself?"

"Donna, we can keep the craft barn open." Mark offered weakly.

"If you don't care about the trees, or the people of Sutton, or your own Papa—think about your mother and father. Don't their lives mean anything to you?"

Again, Mark stood speechless. Several customers entered the farmhouse and approached the counter where Brett was waiting for them. Donna didn't lower her voice.

"Dreams require sacrifice, Mark, but you don't abandon your family. What will the music mean to you if you give up all the wrong things?" She walked away and once out of sight, Mark heard her release a sob.

What could he say? Was she right? Was he abandoning the family? Is that how she and Papa saw it? He stumbled into the chair by the fireplace and put his head in his hands.

Mom and Dad had each other. Natalie wants no part of this farm. Papa will not live forever. And then what will I do?

Hours later, Mark found Papa sitting on a stool by the trees. Wasn't there time to explain the details of the sale and allow Papa to understand—or at least, not be as angry? The setting sun cast a warm glow over the trees, and Christmas carols played steadily from the lot speaker.

Before Mark could reach him, Papa was off the stool and talking to customers. Mark watched him come to life as he talked about the trees. The customers looked spellbound too.

"Christmas miracle . . . Shafer trees," Mark overheard a few of Papa's energetic words. "Believe . . ."

Mark didn't need to hear everything to figure out what Papa was doing. He was desperate and wanted to save the farm, didn't he?

Did I push him to make things up about the trees?

How can I go through with this?

"There's buried treasure, that's why," Papa said to a few young men. Mark strained to hear the rest.

"My great-grandfather settled this land. We've been the only owners for over a hundred years. His treasure is buried on this farm, and the trees are special."

What is he saying now?

Papa moved from one customer to the next, exuberant and animated, no doubt repeating the story of buried treasure. The customers showed varying degrees of interest. Mark couldn't watch any more.

He's lost it. The sooner I sell this place, the better.

Mark found Donna in the craft barn just after closing time. Her eyes were red, but dry. And by the way she greeted him, he could tell her rage had subsided, but not her distress.

"Did you sell out of anything today?" He tried an easy question.

"We're out of Mrs. Shaw's crafts. She's in Oregon visiting her daughter and gave us all she had before she left. I don't know where she found the time to do it and deal with that apartment fire. She's a sweet woman."

"That reminds me. I forgot to mention that I invited some more friends to dinner on Christmas Day," he said.

"Why not? Better invite everyone you can. The last Christmas dinner here should be a big one, right?" she said, a bit cutting and not like Donna at all.

"The farmhouse will still be here. It's the trees—"

"How many did you invite?"

"What? Oh, three. Well, maybe two. Remember Angela from the news story? She and her daughter and maybe her mother."

"Do you mean the one who thought we'd given her money? She doesn't like us, does she? When did you see her again?" Donna asked as she refilled jars with candy-cane pens.

"I delivered a tree, a second one, to her. She's moved to another apartment at Blackstone." He paused. "And she was here Saturday for the hayride event."

"Hmm. And she said yes when you invited her to dinner?" Donna paused. "She's a cute gal. Are you interested in her?"

"What? No!" *I'm engaged to Natalie.*

"She's probably interested in *you*. You invited her for Christmas dinner. She wouldn't say yes unless . . . well, you know."

Mark didn't know. "Her daughter helped convince her." He changed the subject and tried to clarify some things. "Donna, I'm sorry I didn't tell you sooner what I was doing. I had planned to, but there didn't seem to be a good time."

"You're sorry about not telling me sooner . . . that you're selling the farm," she said, "but you're not sorry that you're selling it?" She picked up the broom and started sweeping. The floor took the brunt of her frustration.

"I wish there were another way—I really do. Papa had Nana. My mom and dad had each other."

"Has Natalie pushed you to sell? Is that what this is all about? I knew that girl was trouble. She's trouble, Mark."

"No, she hasn't pushed me. She supports me. She's the only one who can see how much I love music." Mark paused and pushed his hands deep into his pockets. "There's something I don't understand about the trees," he said. "If they *are* 'miracle trees' then what about my parents? They loved this land. Where was their miracle?"

Donna's eyes filled with tears. "I don't have all the answers. I'm sorry your parents . . . I'm sorry you were so young. But if you're asking me that question—what was their miracle? Don't you see? It was you and your sister, Kate. The two of you survived. Besides, you know it's not just the trees, Mark. You have to believe. It's about your faith."

"I didn't mean to upset you again," Mark said. Donna's answer settled over him. He'd never thought of it that way, like surviving was some sort of a—no, he'd always missed his parents too much to think of it like a miracle. But hearing her say it. She was right.

"If you're really going to go through with the sale, I ought to tell you more about your dad. He spent a lot of time learning from Papa." Her face grew more serious.

"Learning what? Planting schedules and pruning routines?"

"Yes, but more than that. I used to see the two of them on their walks sometimes. Your Papa had your dad blindfolded once, had him touching all the trees in a row."

"Donna, Papa has some strange ways. Actually do you know what he's telling the customers tonight? Buried treasure! He's desperate," Mark said as he emptied the garbage into a larger bag. "What am I going to do? Can you have a talk with him?"

Donna stopped sweeping and sat on the stool behind the counter. She wiped her brow and squared her shoulders. "Why me? You're the only one who can tell him what he needs to hear."

"But buried treasure, Donna? Come on. It has to stop." Mark stood and stacked a few empty boxes.

"He's right. That's what your dad found," she said quietly.

"Not you too." Mark groaned. "You can't be serious. If my dad found a treasure then where is it? I just—I can't do this."

"Please, listen."

"Maybe another time. I'm meeting Natalie soon." He left the craft barn as anguish welled up in his chest.

Why would she say that about my dad? If he found a treasure, what did he do with it?

CHAPTER 17

A cold Monday morning wasn't pleasant even with a decent night's sleep, but Angela hadn't slept more than a few restless hours. Mr. Buckley's threat on Saturday filled her with dread for the rest of the weekend. She couldn't be sure of anything he had told her. Would he make good on his threat? Would he evict them if he wanted to? Could he?

One thing she did know—Christmas was in eleven days. How hard would it be to endure the lousy work environment until after the holiday? Then she could quit and find another place to live.

Like that's an easy thing to do.

She would have called Mrs. Shaw if she hadn't been in Oregon. Mrs. Shaw would have told her not to work for him in the first place.

And then there was her mother. Caroline had asked every day since Mark Shafer delivered the second tree when they were going to call Grandma Elliott. Could she ask her mother for advice? What would she say? *What she always says—come home. Come home and admit that I was right and you were wrong.*

She dropped Caroline off at school and returned to the rental office. She sat in her truck, waiting, no need to go inside one more minute before she had to.

Except for the gas I'm wasting.

I can do this . . . for Caroline.

"Good to see you this morning," Mr. Buckley said, sounding like his old self.

Angela smiled politely and looked at her phone to avoid conversation. She found plenty of work to do, and when a couple came in asking to see an apartment, she offered to give them a tour. She felt like she might be able to get through the day after all.

Mr. Buckley usually left for lunch around eleven thirty, and when he returned, Angela took her break. That way, the office could remain open.

"What do you say you and I go get some lunch together?" he said offhandedly.

"What . . . about the office?" she stammered.

"We can put the closed sign in the window for an hour or two. Get your coat." He reached for his and watched her.

Angela continued filing leases and acted as if she didn't hear what he had said.

Think of something.

"There's that new sandwich place we could try." He flipped the sign in the window, and Angela's heart started to race.

"I can stay. I wanted to get some of this work done so I could take off Thursday and Friday next week," she offered faintly.

Mr. Buckley opened his desk drawer and looked for something he didn't find. "We don't have to be long, then." He walked across the office and took Angela's coat off the rack and handed it to her.

"Thanks." She stood and buttoned her coat. Mr. Buckley broke out in a satisfied smile and they walked out of the door together and to his car. As he was unlocking it, Angela spoke up.

"Look, I just got a message from the school and . . . Caroline is in the nurse's office. I need to go pick her up." Angela kept walking and jumped into her truck. She wished she could have seen his face, but she didn't look back. Warm tears burned the corners of her eyes.

She turned the key, the starter dragged, and the engine didn't turn over.

Don't do this, not now!

She didn't look out her window. One more turn and she drove out of the parking lot.

Not exactly a dramatic exit!

She drove toward the school to pick up Caroline so she could feel like she hadn't lied, but her tears stopped as she thought of Mr. Don Buckley, his threats and his what? His dishonesty. It became clear what she wanted—no, what she *needed* to do.

After two calls to directory assistance and some backtracking, she found the Blackstone Apartment Management Office in Millbury near the mall. A freezing rain began to fall as she parked. She looked for her umbrella under the seat—not that it mattered. Her hair had frizzed as soon as she left her apartment that morning.

What can I tell them? I don't have any proof that he's stealing from residents. What about today? Am I going to complain that he asked me to lunch?

She straightened up at the memory of it, got out of the truck and darted into the warm building. The receptionist told her she could not see the owner without an appointment.

"Great. Can I make an appointment?" Angela stood there, a little wet, but undeterred.

"Let me get her book," the receptionist said and rolled her eyes. "What day did you have in mind?" she asked as she flipped pages.

"Today." Angela looked at the time on her phone. "How about one o'clock?"

"That's in five minutes!" The girl picked up the phone and turned as she spoke, then swiveled back with her answer.

"Ms. Sullivan won't be available until two."

"I can wait. Tell her this is Angela Donovan from the Blackstone Apartments—the one with the fire."

Ms. Sullivan was warm and personable, nothing like the receptionist, and she apologized to Angela for the wait. Her kindness changed Angela's aggressive tone to a confessional one. She detailed everything she had observed while working with Mr. Buckley and concluded with the threat and the lunch invitation.

"I was planning to quit after Christmas, but I'm done. I'm going to need to find a new place to live, too."

"You won't need to do any of that," Ms. Sullivan replied. "Thank you for coming here today—it was brave of you."

"I don't know about that."

"We've been *aware* of Mr. Buckley for a while. We have cause to dismiss him," she said in a restrained way.

"I didn't realize." Angela's shoulders dropped with relief. "Do you mean you're going to fire him?"

"Yes. What we don't have is someone to take his place," Ms. Sullivan explained.

The phone rang, and the receptionist came in and put a few more folders on the desk. Angela shifted in her chair and looked at the clock. She had to leave soon to pick up Caroline.

"So, as I was saying, we're interviewing right now for the apartment manager position. Based on what you've told me and given the circumstances, would you be willing to take over as an interim manager? We'll provide you with more training, of course, but this situation has gone on long enough."

"Interim manager? Me?"

"That wasn't what you were expecting, was it? Would you be willing? There is a salary, and rent is free, of course."

"Yes, I'm willing to help. But I have a daughter in school," she said as she looked at the clock. *And a job I'm supposed to be starting there.* "Yes, I can work it out." Angela said more definitively.

Ms. Sullivan thanked her again for coming in. She provided Angela with an application to fill out and return, but told her to plan to start on Wednesday.

"And we'll take care of Mr. Buckley," she reassured her.

Angela drove back to Sutton in sleet mixed with snow but it didn't bother her. Not in the slightest. How could it? Mr. Buckley would be gone. She'd have a salary paying job. And no rent to pay.

CHAPTER 18

Mark and Natalie finished dinner but Mark was still restless. He wasn't satisfied, not with the food, not with the way Papa and Donna found out about the sale and especially not with the way he'd handled it. If he hadn't left the business card on the counter, or if he'd thought of some reason why the surveyors had come, it might have been different. But he hadn't. And the fact that he'd negotiated for the cabin and craft barn did little to help anyone feel good about the deal.

Natalie invited him to her place and they drove in their separate cars to her apartment in Millbury. Unlike previous occasions, Mark didn't find comfort in Natalie's reassurances that he was doing the right thing. He listened silently to her encouragement but this time was different. She hadn't seen the disappointment on Papa's face or seen Donna's swollen eyes.

"They'll adjust. You have to look out for yourself. If you don't go through with the sale, someday it will just be you and the farm. You've told me you can't picture that," she reminded him.

Mark nodded. How could he disagree? He'd said it more than once.

"But what about us?" Mark asked.

"What? What do you mean?"

Mark shifted in his seat and reached for her hand. He chose his words carefully. Maybe, just maybe he'd underestimated her. "If I don't go through with the sale, if I keep the farm and the trees . . . what about us? Could we—would you?" He didn't know how to word it. This was harder than proposing. "Would you give it a try—working the farm together?"

He glanced and saw her mouth slightly open, her eyebrows raised and then he focused his eyes directly across the room on the clock by the door. The longer the silence lasted, the harder it became to sit next to her. He shuffled his feet and released her hand—the hand with the new diamond ring on it.

"Mark, I—I don't know what to say."

His cell phone rang. He might have ignored it, but it was late for anyone to be calling him. He answered, and risked another look at Natalie's face still waiting for an answer.

"Mark? This is Brett. It's not good. Please come . . . we're at UMass Medical, Worcester."

"What? Why Worcester?" Mark sat up straight on the couch.

His phone dropped the call. He dialed back and it went to voicemail.

Mark stood, and tried to call again.

"What is it?" Natalie asked though he was already heading for the door.

"That was Brett." Mark turned to face her. "I'm not sure, but I think they took Papa to UMass Medical. Can you come with me?" he asked.

Before she could speak, before he could think it through, he knew her answer. No, she wouldn't come. No, she wouldn't give the farm a try. If the situation were reversed, he'd already have his coat on and be by her side. Why hadn't he seen it before?

She looked everywhere but at him.

"I guess," she finally said. "Let me get my warmer coat." She walked over to the closet.

"Never mind," he said. *Forget I asked. While you're at it, forget I proposed.*

Mark sped on the turnpike in spite of the snow. He played the music he had written for Natalie.

She doesn't love me.

I couldn't see it until now.

Please be okay, Papa.

The last time Mark saw Papa, he was on the lot, telling customers about the buried treasure. Had he been happy or desperate? Papa's words came rushing back to him. "We sell our trees, not our land."

Mark tried calling Brett back again, but didn't get an answer. He arrived and entered through the ER and stopped at the desk.

"Where can I find Alberto Shafer?" he asked.

"Let me check. Did he come here by ambulance or did someone drive him?"

"I don't know." The seconds felt like years.

"No one here by that name. Would he have used a different one?"

Mark reeled with confusion, panicking that he had the wrong place. He was sure Brett said UMass, Worcester. "No. He's in his late seventies, they brought him here . . . is he . . . Please, no."

"Sir, why don't you come over here and have a seat." The woman pointed to the row of hard plastic chairs.

"I think he came with Brett, a younger man, almost as tall as I am."

"Let me make a call and see what I can find out."

As she dialed, Brett came through a set of doors on the opposite side of the waiting room with Papa walking slowly behind him. Mark rushed to hug him.

"You're okay! What happened? Did they just release you?"

Brett tried to interject. Mark stayed focused on Papa.

"They didn't need to release me. I'm fine. *You'd* better sit down, though."

Mark, more bewildered than ever, sat in the nearest chair.

"Donna died about an hour ago," Papa said quietly.

"What? Donna?" Mark's chest tightened. "How?" he murmured, willing the air through his lungs.

Papa sat next to him and put his hand on his shoulder.

"She suffered a heart attack. They tried everything."

No. This isn't happening.

"Is her husband here?" Mark asked.

"Yes, and so are her daughters." Papa sat stoically. If he had been crying, Mark couldn't tell. Brett remained standing, staring at the ER doors and shaking his head.

Mark thanked Brett for bringing Papa and told him he could go. He and Papa stayed a short time longer to see if they could help

Donna's family. Then they drove back to the farm together, and like the mornings when they walked the lot, neither spoke.

The weight of what Mark had done settled over him. Had Donna cried angry tears when she learned he was selling? How many times had she tried to share with him—what? What did she know? Was there something about his dad and the farm? *Please listen*, she'd begged.

"Papa, I'm sorry." Mark spoke before the grief could consume him.

Three a.m. and no traffic on the turnpike. Had time stopped? Had the world?

"Me too. We'll miss her, won't we?" Papa said gently.

"Yes. But I mean I'm sorry about the way I've acted. I've been wrong. I hurt Donna and you. I'm so sorry. If we hadn't argued, maybe this wouldn't have happened." His voice trailed off.

"Come on now. Something like this doesn't happen because of one day," Papa said.

Mark took the private road to the cabin.

"I'll make a few calls in the morning to put the word out that we'll be closed for a few days," he told Papa.

"That would be best. Doesn't seem right, does it? She was too young. That should have been me in that hospital." He said with a sigh.

"Don't say that." Mark felt a lump in his throat. "You've got to stick around."

He watched Papa walk to the cabin and then around to the back door.

What's he doing now?

Mark rolled down his window when he heard Papa's voice.

"Better come see this, Mark."

He jumped out of the car and caught up to where Papa stood on the edge of the back lot of trees. With nothing but the waning moonlight, he could still see the dark outline and yellow paint of the backhoe tractor right where it couldn't be—in the middle of the trees, dozens of felled trees.

Mark fought competing waves of grief and anger. "No," he yelled. He ran through the wet-packed snow to the rows of stumps. He collapsed over one and hit it with his fist. "How could they do this?" he cried.

He buried his face into the side of his arm. He stood and made his way through the strewn branches and trees. He climbed into the backhoe and tried to start it. Nothing.

"It's outta gas!"

"Come on back, Mark," Papa shouted. "There's not much we can do tonight."

Mark walked over to Papa, who looked like he hadn't even moved.

"Of all the trees. These are the ones we planted after the fire," Mark said.

"I know. I remember."

"I've been the keeper of the trees for less than a month, and look at them." Mark's eyes stung with tears.

"This is my doing." Papa said. "Don't be too hard on yourself."

"What are you talking about?"

"I got carried away, told too many people about the treasure." He hung his head and rubbed the back of his neck. "This mess here is a perfect example of why we look for the believers. We only tell the ones with the light in their eyes," he explained wearily.

Mark listened as he scanned the dark silhouettes of tree stumps and broken limbs. Ruined, so many of them. Years of work and growth, gone.

Papa turned around to walk inside and said, "It doesn't matter now, does it? This is nothing compared to what it will look like after you sell it."

The resignation in Papa's voice hurt more than the devastation. "I don't want to sell anymore," Mark said.

"What did you say?" Papa asked, turning back around.

"I'm not going to sell," he said as he looked Papa in the eye. "I'm going to make this right."

Papa didn't speak for a moment.

"Unless . . . is it too late? Will it take too long to—?"

"To replant? Doesn't matter how long it takes. We did it after the fire and the trees have come back strong. We can do it again. But you have to want it, Mark."

"I do. I finally do." Mark walked to the cabin door with Papa. "I'll need your help, though. You said it yourself—I have a lot to learn."

"That you do."

"One more thing. Donna said something to me about the buried treasure. Is it true? Is there buried treasure on this land?"

"Why else were those vandals out there? They had that backhoe for a reason. See how they tried to dig? Dumb criminals—ground is frozen. Probably wrecked my machinery."

"So where is the treasure?" Mark asked.

"Don't know exactly. I know where it isn't. I have my theories, based on what my father told me." Papa's gaze wondered back over the south ridge of trees.

"So you've never seen it? Donna said my dad found it."

"I don't know 'bout that. He liked looking for it, I can say that. He'd go around at night digging holes and filling them up by morning." He shook his head. "I'll tell you the same thing I told him—I don't have to see the treasure to know it's there."

Papa looked at Mark, and after a long pause, he asked, "Did I hear you right? You said you're not going to sell?"

"You heard right."

Between the clean-up effort and the outpouring of love and sympathy from the community, Mark and Papa didn't get much sleep. The temporary employees pitched in on the back lot. The weather cooperated and allowed them to clear many of the felled trees.

Mark called his sister, Kate. She wasn't planning on making the trip home, but when she learned of Donna's passing, she said she'd find a flight.

"If I can't fly tomorrow, I'll take the red-eye or something. Does it matter what time I get in?" she asked.

"No. Of course not," he said.

"I'm so sorry, Mark. Will the funeral be next Monday?"

"Can you stay that many days?" he asked. He heard a clicking sound on her end of the phone. "Are you typing?"

"I'm checking flights, and I'm going to try to stay through the holiday and help you. If you want me to, that is. It's the least I can do."

"Wow. If you could, that would be great," he said.

"Wednesday flight, arrives 6:20 p.m. in Providence. Will that work?"

"Sure. I can be there. Thanks for coming." He paused. "Hey, Kate, before you go. There's something else I should tell you. And I've got a question that's kind of unrelated to everything else."

"And you're asking my opinion? Fire away."

"I asked Natalie to marry me a few days ago."

"Congratulations. Are you worried that if I come for the funeral, I won't be able to come later for a wedding?"

"No, uh, that's not it. I may have asked her too soon. How do I call it off?" He paused. "What do I say?"

"Well, I'm sure she could understand this is a difficult time," she said.

If that were the only reason. "It's not that. I don't think she loves me," Mark admitted.

Kate was quiet. "Sounds like a mess. I'll have to meditate on that."

"Meditate? Okay. Thanks, see you tomorrow."

CHAPTER 19

Angela spent most of Tuesday unpacking boxes she'd filled with haste. The new apartment had that sparse, just-moved-in feel and there were only ten days until the holiday. Some things could stay packed, like the contents of the junk drawer. But it would be nice to have the essentials. A picture of Caroline from last summer, for starters, her CDS, and probably the can opener. No, definitely the can opener.

She sifted through the box of kitchen gadgets, and on the bottom, under a stack of semi-used cookbooks, she found the electric can opener. One glance revealed two pieces that ought to have been one.

Oh no, this won't do for the dinners I make lately.

She reached for it, fiddled with the broken piece and declared it unsalvageable.

Figures. It was a wedding present, wasn't it? Where will I find the money to buy another one? Oh wait, I'm not paying rent this month.

Or the next.

That thought spurred her on. She finished unpacking a few more boxes. By the time she was done she had a mental list of the presents she could buy for Caroline.

Of course, there were things Caroline wanted that Angela

couldn't buy. Like the family dinner. With her mother. The one and only Mrs. Catherine Elliott. Could there be a harder mountain to move?

I'll do it for Caroline.

Right after I organize my books.

The bookcase sat against the wall next to the new Christmas tree in the spacious family room. Angela sat on the floor cross-legged, sorting books by the number of times she'd read them. If she'd read it more than three times, the book earned top shelf status. The half-read stack of books she relegated to the bottom shelf, but offered consoling words.

"There, there, Don Quixote, I'll join you and Sancho another day."

The un-read books earned the middle shelf. "I bought you so I *will* read you." She muttered to the mismatched collection sporting titles like "The Marriage Cure" and "The Billionaire Down the Street."

She sat close to the branches of the tree, the pine scent wafted around her. She glanced at the tree once, then twice. Mark had carried it through the door, effortlessly if she remembered correctly.

He stood right by that door and invited them to dinner.

And Caroline asked if her grandma could come.

Angela rubbed her temples. I need to make that call. If I wait any longer, she'll use the short notice as reason not to come.

She looked at the clock and grabbed her cell phone to make the call. She'd need to leave soon to pick up Caroline from school.

"Hi, Mom. This is Angela."

"I know it's you. How's Caroline?"

"She's good. We both are. I have some news." She didn't pause for a reply. "I have a new job. I'm the interim manager at Blackstone Apartments. I start tomorrow."

"I didn't know you had that kind of experience," her mother said.

Angela continued, "And as part of the compensation, we can stay in this two-bedroom apartment—for free."

The silence on the phone lasted long enough for Angela to wonder if the call had been dropped.

"Well how did that happen?" she asked.

"It's kind of a long story. I only have a few minutes before

Caroline gets out of school." Angela took a deep breath and continued. "Anyway, I was wondering, and Caroline was too, if you can join us on Christmas Day for dinner."

This would mean she'd have to drive the 30 miles "all the way" to Sutton. And here Angela was, asking her to do it on Christmas.

Is 30 miles too far? We are family, right?

"Will you be cooking?"

"Don't worry, we'll be eating with some friends," Angela explained hesitantly. "Caroline has been begging me to call you. She really wants you to come."

"Well then, what time and what should I wear?" her voice perked up.

"Um, wear whatever makes you comfortable. Can you be here by eleven?"

"Okay, but isn't that early for dinner?"

"That will allow us some time for Caroline to give you a gift."

"Okay, fine, I'll see you at eleven. And this will be *casual?*"

If she knows the dinner is at some tree farm, she won't come.

"Wear whatever makes you feel comfortable, Mom."

"It is Christmas Day. Your friends understand that, right?"

"They certainly do," she said. "We'll see you on Saturday."

"Yes. And . . ." her mother paused.

Angela heard the school bell and watched the children walk out of the school.

"Do *you* want me to come?"

She almost didn't hear the question, as she was straining to find Caroline in the sea of second-graders.

"Yes, of course I do," she answered. *Did I think about it too long?*

"Good. I have an invitation for you too," her mother said.

"What?"

Caroline opened the door and jumped into the truck. Angela waved to her.

"Who are you talking to?" Caroline asked.

Angela covered the phone and whispered "Grandma."

"Hi, Grandma," Caroline yelled.

"Sorry, Mom, what were you saying?" Angela shook her head at Caroline and put the truck in drive.

I'll have angry carpool moms honking their horns at me if I don't move.

"This Saturday night, I'd like to take you and Caroline to see *The Nutcracker,*" she stated more than she asked.

"Wow. That would be *nice*."

"Good. I already have tickets. Does Caroline have a dress, or will I need to buy something new?"

"She has one." Angela hit the brakes, avoiding the bumper of the minivan in front of her.

"So I'll need to pick you up around six o'clock. Will that be a problem?"

"Yes. I mean no. We'll be looking forward to it."

Angela ended the call and navigated out of the school parking lot. Caroline was already asking what they were looking forward to.

"Grandma is taking us to the ballet on Saturday."

CHAPTER 20

Mark left several messages for John Jackson. It wasn't like him to not return his calls. Of course, ever since Mark had agreed to sell, John had been hard to reach. Mark would have driven to the office to talk to him in person, but when he searched for his address, all he could find was a post office box.

Even though the farm was technically closed for another day, they didn't turn away customers who came for a tree. Some showed up who had travelled a good distance and didn't check the website. Papa insisted on handling the transactions himself, and Mark allowed him to use the old cash box. It was either that or Papa was prepared to give the trees away.

"The trees should be free in honor of Donna this week."

"We could do that," Mark countered, "but there are other things we can do, ways that won't result in chaos on the lot. Let's rename the craft barn after her."

"I like that idea," Papa said. "This place might be in good hands yet."

"I've got to leave to pick up Kate. Are you okay here with Brett?"

"'Course I am."

Mark turned back to where Papa was standing and hugged him.

"What are you doing that for? Are you catching a plane while you're at the airport?"

"I'm just trying to say I love you."

"Go on now. I figured as much when you decided to keep the farm."

Before the forty-five-minute drive to the airport, Mark checked his phone for messages from John Jackson. None. Not that he expected business calls, but maybe condolences.

I shouldn't be surprised, should I?

Kate was bundled up head to toe when she got off the plane. Mark could hardly recognize her.

"Are you sleeping outside tonight or what?" he teased.

"Look, it was sixty-five degrees when I left LA this morning. And I thought that was cold," Kate said.

"There's food back at the house, but what do you like these days? Are you still lactose whatever, or vegan something?"

"When you put it like that, maybe we should find a place to eat."

Mark stopped at a trendy restaurant before they left Providence that looked like it might serve what his sister considered food. As they walked to the door, he noticed a black Hummer.

"Please tell me you aren't going to trade in your Beamer for one of those," Kate asked.

"What? No. That just looks familiar," he said.

Could it be? What are the chances?

The hostess led them to a table. Mark scanned the dining room, but the booths made it hard to see who was seated. Halfway to their table, down an aisle, he saw Natalie.

Two more steps and he could see John Jackson sitting next to her. Enjoying his dinner.

The hostess continued walking and Kate slowed, waiting for Mark.

He'd stopped at the edge of their table. The words he had rehearsed to say to John left his mind. New ones formed, probably words he shouldn't speak.

Kate asked, "Are these friends of yours?"

"Kate, I'd like you to meet John Jackson." He motioned to him. "He's the man who has been trying to get me to sell our farm. And this—this is Natalie. At least, I think that's her name." He shot Natalie a look, not a question, but a dismissal.

Natalie sat up straighter in her seat and John slid his arm out from around her shoulders.

"Mark." Natalie began pulling the ring off her hand. "It wasn't supposed to go this far. I had no idea you'd *propose*." She sounded sincere, but mostly embarrassed.

Mark looked from Natalie's face to John's. "You almost did it, John. You almost had me. Was she going to hang on until the deal closed, or maybe wait a little longer to break up and make it look good?" He noticed the couple next to them staring, but he didn't stop talking. "Looks like I'm going to make this easy for you, Natalie. In case you haven't figured it out, I'm not selling any part of my land."

John wiped his mouth with his napkin. "Don't be rash, Mark. You're making a mistake."

"No, no, I'm not."

"We had our own agreement," John said. "You'll need to repay the money I just gave you."

"Yeah. See that ring on your girlfriend's hand? It's all yours. You two are made for each other. Let's go, Kate."

Mark left the restaurant in easy but long strides. As soon as they were out of the restaurant and in the cold air, Kate caught up to him. "Mark, wait. Is she your fiancée?"

"Was. She *was* my fiancée."

"I'm sorry, Mark."

"Saves me the trouble of calling it off." He squared his shoulders and willed it to be true. He wouldn't be sorry.

"But did you like her?" Kate asked, shivering.

"I liked what I thought she was. Turns out she was a fake."
And I almost fell for it. Almost.

"Did you see, what was his name—John? Did you see his face? I think you shut him down."

Mark opened the car door for Kate and nodded, the slightest smile escaped his lips.

"Still, Mark, I'm so sorry you had to run into her like that."

"Don't be. I'm not. At least I didn't sell."

Mark reopened the farm on Friday. He and Papa walked the lot of snow-dusted trees, much like they had dozens of times before. Mark's steps were the same but now his heart was open, maybe for the first time. He looked at each tree like an individual, its size and shape distinct from the next.

Papa slowed and turned to Mark. His features softened as he nodded.

"You did right." He uttered the three quick—but warm—syllables in the chill, morning air.

Gone were the plans with Natalie. Gone were the worries over selling and Papa and buying the house on Hickory. And he never felt better. Now he looked at the trees with interest.

Will this one go to a home with children?

Will this one brighten someone's holiday, maybe someone having a hard time?

As they returned to the farmhouse, Brett was waiting for them with two trees loaded into one of the work trucks.

"There are two families from the fire that have moved into new apartments now," he explained.

"Great," Mark said. "I'll make a call and find out when I can deliver them."

"You delivered the last one," Brett said. "I don't mind going if you're busy."

"I'll make the time. Thanks, Brett." Was it obvious that he had another reason to go? And so what if it was? He found the number for the Blackstone Apartments.

"Hello, can I talk to Mr. Buckley?"

"He is no longer with the company," a woman answered. "May I help you?"

"Angela? This is Mark Shafer. I'm calling from the—"

"Hi, Mark," she said.

"So, Mr. Buckley is gone?"

"Yes. I'm—filling in for a little while. They're calling it 'interim' manager."

"Wow, congratulations," he said. "Hey, it was great to see you at the farm last week."

"Caroline and I had a nice time. Did you need something?"

"Oh, right. I have two more trees for the other families that have moved back in. If I come by today or tomorrow to drop them off, would that be okay?"

"Of course. I've been able to talk to both residents after I talked to Brett. Let me get you those apartment numbers. If you park around by the back entrance, it will be easier to get to building D," she explained. "And thanks again for what you've done."

How did she come by the new position? He almost asked her. And what time would she be there? He lost his nerve somewhere between her words "back entrance" and "building D."

"It's no trouble."

No trouble at all.

CHAPTER 21

Working on Saturday proved to be the only inconvenience of the interim manager position. Thankfully, one of Caroline's friends invited her to a play day, freeing Angela to tackle the files that needed a thorough reorganizing. Mr. Buckley hadn't been the most detail oriented manager. Angela reassured Caroline she'd pick her up later and they'd have enough time to get ready for the ballet.

She opened the rental office and sorted through some mail and paperwork. Her thoughts drifted to Mark Shafer. Had he dropped off the trees to those residents? She couldn't find a trace that he'd been there. Why did it matter? *He has a girlfriend,* she chided herself. She listened to the phone messages for distraction. No use. There was only one week until Christmas and that meant dinner at the tree farm.

Yes, she had agreed to it, but she had no idea what to expect.

Except food, of course. And Mark.

Oh this won't be awkward at all. The things I do for Caroline.

The office door opened and Angela looked up from her desk. Mark strode in, pulled off his hat and ran his hand through his hair. She sat up straighter.

"Okay, those trees are put up," he said.

"Thank you. I'm sure the families appreciate it."

They looked at each other for a moment.

He's different—calmer, maybe.

"So you're the manager now?" Mark asked. "The way you talked at the farm last week, I thought maybe you weren't going to stay around here." He paused. "We've had a few changes at the tree farm. I was going to ask—well, no, maybe now isn't the best time."

"I wasn't planning on this job," she explained. "Mr. Buckley was fired. But what do you mean? What kind of changes?"

"Never mind." He walked back toward the door.

Say something else.

She opened her mouth, not sure what was going to come out of it, but before she could speak, Mark turned around.

"Are you busy tonight?" he asked. "If you're interested, we could take Caroline to see the lights."

My first offer for a real date in a year, and I'm supposed to go the ballet with my mother.

"Yes, I'd love that. But Caroline is going to the ballet," she said without any further details.

"By herself?" Mark asked.

"No—my mother is taking us. I mean *her.*"

"If you have plans, I understand. I thought Caroline would like to see the lights. If she can't come maybe we could go another time?"

"Lights are great. We don't have to tell Caroline what she's missing."

"Okay, then. Can I pick you up at six?"

"Six fifteen?" she asked in a panic. *Mother's never late, but if he's early, that could be bad. She may need to recover when she finds out I'm not going.*

"Sure, six fifteen."

"How about six twenty?"

Now I sound like an auctioneer. My chances for a second date are disappearing.

"There's no rush. I'll come at six thirty," he said and opened the door to leave.

Angela sat up in her chair and watched him go.

And then she remembered.

Doesn't he have a girlfriend? Yes, he has one. What business does he have, asking me on a date? Wait, he suggested the lights for Caroline. What if he's bringing "Nat"? Oh, what have I done?

Once home with Caroline, Angela began cooking a simple dinner while she tried to think of what she could tell Caroline. Was she going to be disappointed?

"There's been a change of plans tonight," she said nonchalantly. "I think it would be best for you and Grandma to go to the ballet, just the two of you."

"Did you have another fight?" Caroline asked immediately.

"What? No." *At least, not yet.* "I really think it would be better if you had your own time with her, without me."

"And Grandma is okay with that?"

"I think so."

I hope so.

Caroline put on her red velvet Christmas dress, the one Angela had found on clearance the previous year. Angela curled Caroline's hair and watched the clock, adding up the minutes she'd have left to make herself look presentable before Mark came.

What will I do if he shows up with Natalie? He wouldn't. Would he?

The doorbell rang and Caroline ran to answer it. Angela followed her.

"Oh, you look beautiful, dear," Cathy said to Caroline. She glanced at Angela. "You aren't coming like that, are you?"

"No."

"Hurry, then. How long do you need to clean up?"

"Uh, I've . . . I'm not feeling my best. I'd better stay home," she answered.

"Well, that's a disappointment. It doesn't feel like the flu, does it?"

"No. That's not it. I can reimburse you for the ticket." She bit her lip, knowing mother the tickets weren't cheap.

"Nonsense. I'd rather you come, but if you're not well, by all means get some rest."

"We get to have time together, just you and me, Grandma." Caroline hugged her, and Cathy looked bewildered.

As soon as they left, Angela raced to her bedroom closet. She had unpacked, but her clothes weren't as organized as they needed to be so she could find a decent outfit. She tried on two different sweaters and settled on a black and gray turtleneck.

What difference does it make? This is probably some kind of pity date anyway.

She ran the flat iron over her hair, not like it wouldn't be frizzy in 20 minutes. Her mother's question, "How long do you need to clean up," rang in her ears. She had applied make-up to one eye when the doorbell rang.

Great. Give me two seconds.

She finished the other eye and the doorbell rang again.

"Coming," she called.

When she finally opened the door, she could see relief on Mark's face. He was more dressed up than the jeans he'd been wearing two hours ago.

"Hi, sorry. I didn't mean to keep you waiting. Come on in."

He stepped in and she returned to her room and grabbed her coat and purse. She ignored the mirror when she walked by it.

Nothing I can do about it now.

"Have you already had dinner?" he asked.

"No, but that doesn't mean you—"

"Neither have I. Let's get something to eat," he said.

Mark opened the passenger door of his BMW for Angela. "Is that a sunflower purse?" he asked. "That's unique."

"Caroline picked it out. She has a better fashion sense than I do, I'm sure." *Fashion and Caroline—what else can we talk about?* "This is a nice car." She said as he started it.

"Thanks. I'm thinking about trading it in. I need a truck." He explained more about work at the farm. No mention of Natalie. Was that a good sign?

They arrived at the restaurant, and while they waited for their food, Angela asked Mark what he had meant at the rental office.

"Were you going to ask me something earlier? You mentioned there were changes at the farm."

"Oh, yeah, about that. My sister is in town so we should be okay, but when she returns to California, we will need help in the craft barn," he said quietly.

"Doesn't Donna run that?"

"She did." He hesitated. "Donna passed away on Monday."

"Oh, I'm sorry to hear that. Really, Mark. Was it sudden?"

"Yes, very. A heart attack. We closed for a few days and then we'll close again on Monday for her funeral. That's why my sister came, why she's staying an extra week."

Their food arrived, and Mark stared down at his plate. "I'm sorry. We don't have to talk about all this."

Angela sat back in the booth and noticed his furrowed brow and strong features. Even though he had a weathered complexion there was a softness around his eyes.

"Please don't apologize. I don't mind," she replied. "Thank you for telling me. You must have cared about her."

Mark looked appreciative. "Donna's like my second mother. She's been there, well, she was there at the farm ever since my parents died. Just a few weeks ago she told me some things about my parents I'd never heard before." He pushed his food around. "Do you mind—am I talking too much?"

"Not at all." She said. "Go on."

"I didn't plan to share this," he said. "But she wanted to tell me things—I don't even know what they were—I didn't listen. The worst thing is that she's gone and I can't tell her I'm sorry. I can't tell her I'm keeping the farm." He took a long drink from his glass.

Angela had finished most of her food, and a few quiet moments passed between them.

"The *worst* thing would be if you weren't sorry," she said, "or if you still sold the farm."

He looked at her and put his drink down. "Thank you for saying that," he said, "and for listening. You're done with your plate—I'd better stop talking and finish my food."

"Wait," she said. "What will you do about your music?"

Mark looked out over the dining room of the restaurant. "I don't know. I'm not giving it up, but I'm okay with taking a break for a while. Thanks for asking. If you're done, we can go see the lights," he said.

"That was nice of you to think of Caroline." Angela paused. "We don't have to go, if you wanted to bring her." She looked around at the emptying tables.

"I wanted to bring *you*," he said as he stood up.

Speechless, Angela returned his smile with a half-surprised, half-pleased grin.

He parked outside the Enchanted Village and Lights Festival just south of Worcester.

"Look at all this . . . Caroline would definitely be jealous if she knew I was here," Angela said.

"Oh, so you really didn't tell her?" Mark asked as they walked through a well-lit archway.

"Are you kidding? You've heard the way she announces everything," she said. "If she knew I was . . ." Her voice trailed off.

Was what? What is this?

"On a date?" Mark asked, raising his eyebrows.

He said it, not me. But he did say it, right?

"Right. She'd find a way to tell the whole world, or least everyone we know."

"Where is her dad, if you don't mind me asking?"

"He left six years ago. We used to see him here and there, but his parents moved to Florida," she said.

"Let me guess. He moved with them?"

"Yes, he and his second wife live with his parents. And I'm fine with that. Caroline wonders about him, though."

"But she wouldn't mind if you . . . ?"

Angela looked at Mark quickly and then back at the village houses. "If I went on a date," she finished his sentence this time. "No, she wouldn't mind at all."

Every question Mark asked increased Angela's curiosity. "Can I ask *you* a question? Don't you have a girlfriend?" The words were hard to form. Would the night come to an abrupt end with his answer?

"Not anymore." His step quickened.

"Oh, so it's—she's . . . ?"

"Yep, over and gone." Mark smiled. "It didn't work out, and that's for the best." He looked back at Angela.

She took interest in the miniature moving train passing by, unable to meet his eyes. At least the air was cold enough so she could blame it for her red cheeks.

"So can I ask, was that her choice or yours?"

"Let's see. Her boyfriend turned out to be the man who's been trying to get me to sell the farm. She didn't bother to mention that even when I proposed to her."

Angela's eyes widened at the word propose. "I'm sorry, that's awful."

"That's why I said it was for the best. I'd feel sorry too, except once I realized how fake she'd been, I don't know, it made the whole thing easier to move on, I guess." Mark pushed his hands deeper into his coat pockets.

"All this was happening and then Donna's passing, too?"

"Are you wondering why I'd ask you on a date at a time like this?" Mark asked.

Angela navigated around some children. "Maybe. A little."

"Don't take this the wrong way, but from the first night we met on the lot, I wanted to know who you were, I couldn't stop thinking about you. If Donna's passing has taught me anything, it's not to put off . . . " Mark stopped walking. He looked to Angela, scanned the lights and the crowds and then back to her. "I don't want to miss another good thing in life."

There it was. The warmth in his eyes, the sincerity in his feelings, she couldn't argue with that.

They crossed to the other sidewalk and returned to the parking lot. Mark commented on the way the village was constructed. He said they had considered building something like that on the farm one year, but Papa had decided not to do it. He wasn't sure why.

"I like your farm the way it is. There's a good feeling there," she said.

"Coming from you, that's quite a compliment," he said, "So Papa's talk of miracle trees doesn't bother you anymore?"

"I've been thinking about that." She paused. "When I was young, the day my dad brought the tree home and put it up, the entire house felt different. It *was* magical in a way," she said.

"Is that one of your favorite memories?" he asked. "Your eyes light up when you talk about it."

"Yeah, maybe it is."

He drove back to her apartment. He put the car in park, but hadn't turned off the engine. She started to say "thank you," but at the same time Mark asked, "Can I see you again?"

"Aren't we still coming over on Christmas Day?"

"Yes, of course, but I mean just the two of us."

"Maybe we shouldn't impose, with your family in town and everything."

Just the two of us, he did ask that right? What do I say?

"Please come. It's just my sister. It won't be the same without Donna, but I've been looking forward to you coming."

She met his eyes.

There's that genuine look again.

He leaned and kissed her on the cheek first. Oh so near to her lips. She closed her eyes and his lips brushed over hers. She didn't move, but her hand gripped the door handle.

Her eyes fluttered open as she shifted in her seat. Out of the corner of her eye she could see Caroline and her mother walking towards the door of her apartment!

So close.

"Sorry, I've got to go." She opened the car door, breathless. "Um, thank you, for dinner and everything." She looked one last time at Mark, not wanting to leave.

Angela ran to catch up to her mother and Caroline, who were waiting by her apartment door.

"Feeling better, I see." Her mother said with a grin.

CHAPTER 22

L ate Monday afternoon, Mark waited for the heavy pain in his chest to lift as he and Kate drove away from the church and back to the tree farm. It didn't. Funerals had a way of reminding him of his parent's death, but Donna had been a second mother. He wasn't remembering the pain, he was reliving it.

And compounding it with guilt. Nothing he'd yet could shake the fear that he'd upset her, he'd pushed her too far.

Donna's family and friends would arrive shortly, at Mark's invitation. Where else would they gather to honor her? This is where she'd spent so much of her life.

After he greeted her daughters and visited with her husband, Mark retreated to the kitchen where a few of the catering employees were busy replenishing appetizer trays. That was Kate's doing. She called in a favor from an old boyfriend.

Mark had a crab-stuffed mushroom in his hand when Kate found him near the window.

"There you are. You've had enough of the crowd too?" she asked.

"Long day." He took a bite.

"At least you have something to talk about with these people. All my memories are from like, ten years ago." She looked around the kitchen, "Where did you get that?"

He pointed to a tray about to be whisked out of the kitchen; she grabbed two mushrooms off of it.

"That could be a blessing. At least you didn't devastate her, like I did," Mark said as he looked away.

"Are you still beating yourself up about that? Come on, Mark. You can't take the blame here," Kate started to reassure him.

"You don't have people telling you that you were the son she never had. It makes it worse you know." He finished his mushroom. "I tell you what, though, if our old basketball court wasn't covered with snow and ice, I could go for a game of horse with you right now—blow off some steam."

"That reminds me. Where did you go Saturday night after you asked me to close? It's a good thing I had Brett here."

"Would you be mad if I told you I went out on a date?" He kept a straight face.

"A date? You don't waste any time!" Kate poured a drink for both of them. "Do I know this girl? Or do I need to?"

"Remember the news story, the one about the woman who got the money, and then she tried to give it back?"

"You took her out? How did that happen? I thought she didn't like the farm."

"That was before the apartment fire. Then I delivered a tree to her." He paused to take a drink.

"Wait, this is the same girl—you lost me. What's her name?"

"Angela." A smile broke out on his face.

"Aw, look at you. You like her," Kate teased.

"I wouldn't have asked her out if I didn't."

"But really, you look love-sick."

"Cut it out." He set down his glass and grabbed a dishtowel. "I still remember how to use this," he joked.

"So what do you like about this Angela?" she asked.

"Forget it. I'm not saying anything else."

"Oh, come on. You're tougher than that." She grabbed another dishtowel. They began snapping them at each other and playing harder with every hit and miss. "You must be smitten if you're not talking."

"Nice try," he said. "She's amazing. How's that?"

"Ouch." She laughed and shot back. "And you know this from what, one date? You're such a guy!"

133

"First of all, she's the kind of person who doesn't put up with any nonsense."

"Ha—then what does she see in you?"

"Thanks. Hey, watch it." A glass pitcher wobbled on the counter. Kate got in another hit, they both laughed. Papa walked into the kitchen.

They stopped and tried to compose themselves, like they were kids again and caught with their hand in the candy jar.

"Sorry, Papa," Mark muttered.

"For what? Looks like I found the party. Donna would have joined you in here and been whipping the both of you," he said. "Now settle down and come say good-bye to the guests."

Mark stood near the front door and shook hands and offered hugs. Donna's daughter, Jill, walked over with a short, older woman.

"Mark, this is someone I'd like you to meet." She motioned to the woman. "This is Mrs. Shaw."

"So you're the famous Mrs. Shaw. Your crafts are some of our bestsellers," he said. "I'm glad to finally meet you. Donna loved working with you."

"I just can't believe it. I'm so sorry," she said. "I came as soon as I heard, as soon as Jill called."

"That's right. You were in Oregon?"

"Yes. I want to help any way I can. Jill said I should talk to you about the craft barn."

"If you're still looking for someone to help run it," Jill said to Mark, "look no further than Mrs. Shaw."

"Well, no one can take Donna's place. But I will do what I can," she said.

Mark scanned the room for Kate. "Let me find my sister. If you have some time, we can talk about this."

He found Papa and Kate and visited with them for a few minutes. They both agreed that Mrs. Shaw would be a great fit.

"While you're at it, see if she'd like to come for Christmas dinner," Papa said.

"Are you sure?" Mark asked. "I've already invited Angela and her family. Without Donna here—no offense to you, Kate—can we handle it?"

"She left her family in Oregon to be here," Papa said. "It doesn't hurt to ask."

More people filed out of the farmhouse. Mark and Mrs. Shaw sat by the fireplace and talked about the craft barn and Donna. Toward the end, he invited her over for Christmas dinner.

"I'm honored," she said.

"I can't say it will be as nice as it usually is, but we'd love to have you join us, unless you have other plans."

"No, I don't. What can I bring?

"That's not necessary," Mark started to explain, but he didn't get very far.

"Now, listen here, I'm not to be entertained like a child. I'll come so long as I can cook something. I'm no match for Donna, but I'll bring a little bit of England with me."

"That's generous of you." Mark said.

"Pshaw. No trouble. It's a privilege. How many will be eating?

"I—" Mark stammered, and Kate arrived.

"Mark, have you arm-wrestled this poor woman into cooking for us?" she teased.

"No, I . . . she offered." He held up his hands in innocence.

"He's right. I insisted," Mrs. Shaw said.

"There will be six—seven, including you," Mark said.

Kate continued, "We'll be here cooking too."

Once Mrs. Shaw left and the door closed, the finality of the day settled around Mark. He and Kate and Papa milled around the kitchen, cleaning up. No one spoke. Kate put the last of the utensils in the dishwasher. *She'll return to California soon enough.* And Papa, he swept the kitchen floor slowly, with bent shoulders. *Was he tired?*

How are we going to celebrate Christmas—let alone run the farm— without Donna?

Mark wrestled the last trash bag closed. "Well, Papa, I'm thankful you suggested we invite Mrs. Shaw for dinner," Mark said. "Otherwise, we'd be eating Kate's Tofurkey on Christmas Day."

"And you'd love it," she shot back.

CHAPTER 23

What use was a date if you couldn't talk about it with girlfriends? Angela's choices were a highly opinionated mother and a much-too-young daughter—even if she was too smart for her own good. But she had to say something to answer their wide, expectant eyes.

For Caroline's explanation, she'd been to the Enchanted Village with a friend, and yes, Angela would take her there. Her mother's curiosity would have to wait until Caroline was asleep. That would give her some time to think through the narrative for potential points that would disclose too much information.

Anything you say can and will be used against you. What, am I still sixteen? I can tell her what I did, how it went. We're both adults. I just won't name names. At least, not last names. We have Christmas dinner to get through.

No, her mother would not know that they would be spending part of Christmas Day with the same man who had taken her to dinner.

"What does he do for work?" Cathy asked.

Angela answered quickly. "He's in the agriculture business."

"That's a departure from Todd," she said. "How did you say you met him?"

"Sutton is small place. We kind of kept running into each other," Angela said as she poured hot water into two mugs.

"Do I get to hear what else you did on your date?" her mother asked.

"We went to see some Christmas lights after dinner."

"How nice, did he hold your hand?"

"Mom, seriously. What kind of a question is that?" Angela got up from the table and put her drink on the counter. She began loading the few dishes from the sink into the dishwasher.

"A reasonable one. I'm trying to figure out what kind of a man he is," she said. "Besides, I don't know what kids do these days."

"I'm almost thirty." Angela laughed. "And no, he didn't hold my hand. It wasn't that kind of date."

"What does that mean? What kind of a date was it?" Cathy carried her mug to the sink and waited.

Okay, so it was the almost-kissed-me kind.

"Um, it was a first date, that's all." But the heat rose in her cheeks as she thought of the way he leaned in, how close he felt . . .

"He asked to see me again," she said out loud.

"And?"

"That's when I saw you and Caroline at the door." *And missed the kiss.*

Angela closed the dishwasher and walked toward the living room. She looked at the decorated Christmas tree and shook her head.

A new apartment, a date with Mark, and my mother and I talking about it, together.

Angela changed the subject. "Do you ever see Florinda?" She walked over to the nativity set across the room where Caroline had put it up, still missing the little lamb.

"Florinda, your piano teacher? Let's see, it's been years and years." Her mother picked up her coat and paused before she put it on.

"The last I knew, she returned to Portugal to be with her mother for a time. I'm not sure if or when she came back," she said. "You were fond of her, weren't you?"

Angela checked her mother's face for signs of jealousy, but she couldn't detect any.

"She was a good teacher, you know, she cared."

"I could ask around if you'd like. I'd better go now. Providence is a long—."

"Drive." Angela finished the well-worn sentence. "I know Mom. Thanks, for coming tonight and taking Caroline." She walked over to the door. "I'm glad you two had some time together."

"Me too," Cathy said. "Maybe next time I come, I can meet—what was his name?"

"It's Mark." *Mark Shafer. But you don't need to know that.*

The last day of school before Christmas break, Angela arranged for a long lunch so she could shop for Caroline. She headed to the mall in Millbury unsure if she would have enough time and money to find what was on her list.

She browsed the sweaters first and then looked at backpacks. On her way to the toy department, she walked by the jewelry counter, and a gem-studded necklace caught her eye. Expensive, no doubt, but a necklace Caroline would love. The saleslady appeared and mentioned they were running a fifty-percent-off sale.

"Great. I'll take it."

She checked the time and made her way out of the mall. There was a specialty gift shop with assorted Christmas decorations in the display window. Angela stopped and looked. So many elaborate nativity sets.

Oh, that's right. The lamb!

She walked into the store, and the pine smell filled her senses. Real pine, not artificial, like walking through the trees at the Shafer farm.

She admired each of the nativity sets. One was ornate and painted, with oversized pieces. Another set was hand-carved olive wood—both were expensive. Of all the options, none matched the size or style of hers.

I'm sure Florinda brought it from Portugal.

She picked up a lamb from a set. Could it pass as a match? She was sure it was too big, and when she saw the price, she decided she'd keep looking for a better fit, and a less expensive one.

The necklace will have to do, and I still need to find an Easy Bake Oven.

Angela had promised Caroline they would shop for presents for

Cathy on Thursday after work. That was before she was worn out from a very long day at the rental office. The woman in apartment six called to report that someone had broken her kitchen window. Angela spent half the day coordinating the replacement. For all the perks of the job, there were a few headaches.

They searched several stores looking for something Caroline could give her grandmother. Angela said no to the apron with the words "I love my grandma's cooking" on it, and then had to spend the next ten minutes explaining to her daughter what it meant to have a personal chef.

Shopping for a woman who could buy whatever she pleased was quickly draining the fun out of the whole 'joy of giving' plan. Angela brought Caroline to the specialty shop as a last resort.

"What about this music box?" Caroline asked. She opened it, and "Joy to the World" began playing. There was a small figurine arrangement of Mary, Joseph and the baby Jesus inside. "I love it. Can we give it to her?" Caroline begged.

My mother and "Joy to the World?"

Angela looked at the price and then her watch. She bit her lip instead of protesting. Yes, she could get it. It was pricy but they wouldn't have to visit another store.

While waiting to check out, Angela kept an eye on Caroline as she wandered to the back corner of the store. She returned with a vase full of artificial flowers.

"Where did you find that?"

Caroline pointed to a shelf in the corner.

"On the clearance rack?"

Angela knew her mother wouldn't even be able to pretend she liked it. She'd start by naming each room in her house and get that puzzled look on her face. She'd declare how impossible it would be for them to coordinate with any of her artwork, or pillows or latest wall texture.

"The music box is all we can afford."

"Not for Grandma—for the Shafer family. We can't show up empty-handed, can we?"

She has a point.

"You're right, but it isn't very Christmas-ey," Angela said.

"But I like it. Besides, that's probably all they ever get is holiday stuff. I'm sure they don't have anything like this."

I'm sure they don't.

CHAPTER 24

On Christmas morning Angela woke up to Caroline's whisper-singing a medley—more like a mash-up—of her favorite carols and holiday songs.

"You're a pretty clever alarm clock, you know that?" Angela sat up and motioned for her daughter to come over for a hug.

"Let's go. I've put the baby Jesus in the manger with the rest of the pieces," Caroline said. "And the stockings Mrs. Shaw gave us are full."

Angela grabbed a quilt from the end of her bed. They sat together on the carpet near the tree, with the quilt wrapped around their shoulders. The tree lights glowed gently in the pre-dawn darkness.

"Here, open mine first," Caroline said as she handed her mother a small, soft present.

Angela didn't recognize the wrapping paper. She uncovered a white hand-knit scarf. "When did you do this?" she asked.

"Mrs. Shaw has been teaching me how to knit. She helped me make this one. Do you like the yarn? It has glitter in it!"

"I do. It shimmers like the snow. Thank you. It must have taken you hours. Oh, thank you." Angela said, looking at her daughter with love and making a mental note to thank Mrs. Shaw later.

"Here. I have a few things for you."

Caroline unwrapped the first present from her mother. It was the Easy Bake Oven she had asked for. Next, she held up a small present and shook it gently by her ear.

"What is this?" She discovered a small jewelry box with a necklace inside. "It's beautiful," she exclaimed, holding it up. "It's a Christmas tree! With gems! Thank you, Mom, I love it." She hugged her mother.

Angela held onto Caroline for a minute. "You asked me a while ago, if I did, you know, believe in miracles." Angela paused to stay composed. "And I wanted to make sure you knew." Her words caught in her throat.

"That you believed? Of course I knew. You're the best, mom." Caroline hugged her again, smiling and self-assured. Like she never doubted it. Like she'd never been worried about it at all.

"We better get ready." Caroline said after the hug.

"Right, your grandmother does like to show up early."

Caroline ran to the door and opened it wide, allowing a gust of bitter cold air into the room. Her grandmother stood with her purse on one arm and a bag of gifts in her other hand. She wore a long, red wool coat.

"I like your dressy boots," Caroline said as she stared in awe.

"Please come in, Mom." Angela hurried to the door.

Caroline still needs to learn a few things about her grandmother, like she'd stand there for an hour waiting for an invitation.

"I'll put your coat on my bed. We don't have a place to hang it yet." Angela quickly made her bed and laid the coat on it. When she returned to the family room, Caroline had already given her grandmother their presents.

"We picked these out for you." She beamed.

Angela noticed the mild surprise on her mother's face.

Cathy opened the smaller package first and held up an ornament. It was a small figure of a Christmas caroler that sang when the string was pulled.

"That's from my mom," Caroline said. "She says the music ones are hard to find."

"She's right. Thank you—it's lovely." Their eyes met, and Angela saw for the briefest moment—something like peace, or was it acceptance?

Next, she opened the square, colorfully painted music box, and the distinct notes of the carol spilled out. Cathy looked up at Caroline and then back to Angela.

Please, Mom, don't find fault with her gift.

"How did you know I collect these?" she asked, astonished.

"I didn't," Angela said. "Caroline picked it out."

"You collect music boxes that play 'Joy to the World?'" Caroline asked. Angela and her mother both laughed.

"I collect music boxes, but I don't have one like this. Thank you. It's perfect," Cathy declared and looked at the box for a few more moments. "What's gotten into me? I have your gifts right here." She pulled out the packages and handed them over, and then settled into the sofa.

Caroline was on the floor and Angela sat nervously in the old chair she couldn't bear to throw away. They looked at each other, not sure who should open their gifts first.

"Go ahead," Angela told her daughter. She could see the anticipation in her eyes.

There were three gifts for Caroline. The first was a set of leather-bound books, a deluxe collection of the Anne of Green Gables series.

"You like to read, I hope," her grandmother said.

"Yep, love to. Thank you."

Next was a charm bracelet.

Angela almost asked if those were real gemstones in the charms. *Yeah, if they're from Cathy, they're real!*

"I love it!" Caroline exclaimed. She put it on her wrist and began opening the last gift.

Cathy sat forward on the edge of her seat. "I'm not sure about this one," she said to Angela under her breath.

Caroline opened a square gift box and pulled out some tissue paper. Under it all was the figure of a small lamb. She grabbed it and dropped everything else. She stood up and held it so her mother could see.

"A lamb, a little lamb!" She ran to the table where the nativity was set up. "We're missing one just like this. Come look, Mom. It fits."

Angela walked over in shock, picked up the piece, and examined it.

"I didn't know you were missing one." Cathy said. "Your mother used to carry around a lamb like that. Maybe it's a strange gift, but when I saw it, I thought of you. I hoped you would like it," she told Caroline.

Angela stared at her. How could she remember that? And how could she find a lamb so similar?

"Where did you buy this?" She had to ask.

"That's not the most polite question." Cathy fiddled with the collar on her blouse.

"But I looked. I couldn't find anything that even remotely matched this set."

"I didn't buy it, if you must know. I found it on the ground the night of the fire. I don't know how I saw it, to be honest. I nearly stepped on it. It was filthy—there was so much soot."

"It's the same one. It's your little lamb," Caroline exclaimed. She ran and hugged her mother and then her grandmother. Angela watched her mother stiffen and then slowly return the hug.

"Now it's yours," Angela said to Caroline. She looked to her mother and whispered a thank you.

"You'd better open your present," Cathy said.

Angela picked up the square gift. Due to the size and shape, she assumed it was a music CD.

She opened it and read the title, "Christmas Memories of Home, Volume II."

"Thanks, Mom. I don't have this one." *Kind of not my taste, or hers.*

"That's a small gift, but it goes with something else I have to give you," Cathy added.

That was one of her mother's loaded hints.

"What did you do? You didn't set up another audition for me, did you? I haven't been in the studio for years, Mom."

"No, nothing like that. You'll see what I mean. It's on the other side of Sutton."

What is she up to?

"Did you buy a new car?" Angela asked.

"Now don't ruin the surprise. And don't protest. This is a gift that you can't return—at least, not easily." She flashed a self-satisfied grin. "And it's not new—it's quite used, actually, but you needed something someone couldn't take away from you."

Angela laughed at that comment. If someone wanted to take

her truck, they were welcome to it.

"But I can't let you give me—" *She couldn't have! Well, she could. She didn't! Not a car!*

"It's done. You don't have to worry about it. Of course, I purchased it before I knew you'd gotten your new job, but you'll be able to work that out."

"When can we go see it?" Caroline asked.

"There's not time before dinner. It's almost noon. Are your friends coming? And dinner isn't going to be here, I can see." She motioned over to the empty kitchen.

"No, my friends aren't coming here. We're going there. We'd better go."

Angela's mother offered to drive, but Angela didn't feel like arguing about traffic lights and lane changes on Christmas Day.

"It will be tight with three of us, but Caroline can fit here in the middle."

Angela drove by the dairy farm and the road narrowed.

"Where do your friends live?" her mother asked.

"We'll be there soon." Angela checked her watch.

The road curved, and there was the large, green tree-shaped sign for the turn-off.

"Shafer Family Christmas Tree Farm," her mother read aloud. "I can't believe it. Would you look at that?"

"What?" Caroline asked.

"Angela, your friends aren't the Shafers, are they?"

Caroline cheerily explained their connection. "Sort of. This is where we came to get our Christmas tree, our first tree. You know the one we had in our other apartment, before the fire? Anyway, that tree, we got it for free. Did my mom tell you that? There wasn't anything wrong with it, but my mom didn't want to move it to our new apartment."

"What are we doing *here?*" Cathy asked as they neared the parking lot.

"I'm getting to that part," Caroline said.

"We've been invited to dinner." Angela felt a wave of nerves. Should she have told her mother sooner?

"Hey, I was about to tell her," Caroline continued. "Like I was saying, Mr. Buckley—who isn't a very nice man, but he did do one good thing—he called the farm and asked them to bring another tree to us because of the fire. They were donating trees."

"I can't . . . you didn't say anything about the Shafers," Cathy stammered.

"Mom, it's okay. Caroline asked if you could come—it's all she's wanted for Christmas." Angela put the truck in park and gathered her purse. She looked at Caroline holding the vase of flowers and sighed. "Are you sure you want to bring those?" she asked her daughter, sounding as uncritical as she could.

"Yes, I am," Caroline said.

Cathy hadn't moved.

Is she really going to do this?

"Mom, I'm sorry I didn't tell you sooner. I promise they said it was okay."

"That's true. When Mr. Shafer delivered the tree, the second tree, he invited us." Caroline continued to narrate as Cathy finally opened her door. "I asked if I could bring you, and he said he'd like that. So they're expecting you."

Cathy continued to mutter as they walked a few steps. "I don't believe this. I can't do this."

"What is it, Mom? What's so bad about it? Is it because it's a farm?"

They neared the porch steps.

"I went to high school here. I've met this family," Cathy finally admitted.

Angela's voice rose. "You lived in Sutton . . . in high school?" She stopped walking and lowered her voice. "You never told me that. Is this going to be a problem?"

Caroline ran up the stairs, knocked on the door, and turned around.

"And I dated Greg Shafer." Cathy blurted, red faced. Angela had never seen her mother more terrified.

"You did what?" Angela glared at her mother. *Dated a Shafer?*

"Who is Greg?" Caroline asked.

"Have you been here before?" Angela's mind raced.

Cathy's eyes scanned the farm and rested on the door. "Yes. Some thirty years ago."

CHAPTER 25

Mark opened the front door of the farmhouse. Relief flooded him as he saw Angela standing there with reddened cheeks and the winter sunlight filtering through her curly hair. Her daughter stood next to an older woman. Was this Angela's mother? And why did she look stunned?

"Welcome, and Merry Christmas! I'm glad you could make it." He motioned for them to come in.

"Here, these are for you. Thank you for having us today." Caroline held out the vase.

"Thanks. You didn't have to do that," he said. "These will be great on the table. I love sunflowers."

They walked in and hung their coats on a rack. Mark and Angela's eyes met for a moment before she nervously looked away.

"Please get comfortable." Mark invited them to sit by the fire while he and Kate finished up in the kitchen.

"Do you need any help?" Angela asked.

"No, we're almost ready." He looked again at the older woman and reached out his hand to introduce himself.

"We haven't met. I'm Mark—"

"Shafer," she said the name at the same time he did. "You look just like your father."

An audible moan escaped Angela's lips.

"What was that?" Mark asked.

"Pardon me. I went to high school with—do you know a Greg Shafer?"

"Yes, that's my dad. Excuse me, did you know him?"

"Mark, this is my mother, Cathy Elliott," Angela said a little late.

"Yes. Yes I did."

The room fell silent. Mark looked to Angela and back at her mother. "It's great to meet you." He finally said. "Please, make yourselves at home. I'm going to check on the food."

Mark walked to the kitchen at the back of the farmhouse through the dining room. He set the vase of flowers on the table. It didn't match the cream linens and the holly-themed dishes, but he smiled at the bright yellow flowers.

Mom would have loved them.

He found Kate in the kitchen with Mrs. Shaw.

"That is so strange," he said.

Kate handed him a crystal pitcher. "Put this on the table."

"You know Angela, who I've been telling you about? Her mother is here." He walked into the dining room, set down the pitcher, and back to the kitchen. "She said she went to school with Dad."

"In Sutton? Here, put these on too." She held out two bowls, one filled with roast potatoes and the other with red cabbage.

"Ah, Papa's favorite," he said as he held up the bowl of cabbage.

"It wouldn't be Christmas without it," Papa said as he entered behind Mark.

"What's her name?" Kate asked Mark when he returned to the kitchen.

"Who?" Papa asked.

"Angela's mother." Kate clarified.

"I think she said 'Cathy Elliott'."

"*The* Cathy?" Mrs. Shaw asked as she pulled the turkey from the oven. The pan clanged on the counter. "This won't be as good as Donna's turkey, but my roast potatoes should be the tops. Do you mean the Cathy your sister was named after?"

"You were named after someone Dad went to school with?" Mark asked, bewildered.

"Donna told me I was named after the Cathy Dad had planned to marry," Kate said.

"And Mom was *okay* with that?"

"I guess they were all friends," Kate said. "Are you going to leave Angela and her mom out there alone?"

"They're okay. I think I was making them nervous," he said.

"Oh, please!" Kate teased.

"She can't be the same one, can she?" Mark said. "Mrs. Shaw, how do you know all this?"

"I knew Donna for years, son. We talked about everything. That's what women do," she said as she arranged the turkey platter.

"We're talking about Sutton High in, what, 1967 or '68? How many other girls named Cathy could there be?" Kate didn't stop moving, setting up the serving dishes.

"I remember that girl," Papa said. "I'll go meet her and ask her what—"

"No, Papa, let's not bring it up, not today." Mark said.

"She was a fancy girl, if I remember right." He leaned against the counter and ate a few grapes from the bowl. "I met their family one Christmas. Her father was a politician."

"Let's get through this dinner with as little drama as possible," Mark said.

"Fine by me," Mrs. Shaw said. "We have to move this food or we aren't going to have a dinner at all."

They finished carrying all the food to the dining room. Mark invited Angela and her family to join them. He introduced Kate and Papa, and kept talking to ensure that Papa didn't try to interview Cathy.

"Mrs. Shaw," Angela exclaimed. "How wonderful to see you here!"

"What a pleasant surprise. Mark, you didn't tell me it was *my* lovely Angela."

"You two know each other?" Mark rubbed his forehead.

"She babysits me," Caroline piped up.

"Thank you for coming to be with us. We're smaller in numbers today." He paused and looked at Papa. "But we're thankful to be together, and for your friendship."

"I'll say grace," Papa said.

Mrs. Shaw wiped her eyes with a handkerchief. "That was lovely. Okay, everyone, let's pull our crackers."

"Oh yay!" Caroline said. "I've been waiting for this."

"Here." Mrs. Shaw held up the brightly colored paper tube from her own plate and demonstrated. "That's right, cross your arms with your neighbor and you each pull an end—there!"

The trinkets and goodies erupted after the popping and cracking sounds, followed by everyone's laughter.

"Now enjoy," she said.

The serving dishes were passed and plates were filled. Courteous and predictable words were exchanged until Caroline spoke.

"So where is your girlfriend?" she asked Mark with perfect eight-year-old curiosity.

"She . . . um," Mark stuttered and looked at Angela.

"He doesn't have one anymore," Kate said, and shot Mark a "you-can-thank-me-later" look. "So, Caroline, what did you receive for Christmas?"

"My mom gave me this necklace I'm wearing." She held it up to show it off. "It's a pine tree, a very sparkly one. And my grandma gave me this bracelet. She gave me books and a lamb, too."

"Will the apartments let you have a pet lamb?" Papa asked and winked at her.

"Not a live one—a small one for our nativity set," she said and giggled. "And my grandma gave my mom a car."

All eyes were on Angela.

"My truck, um, needs a lot of work." Angela stammered.

"I didn't give you a car," Cathy said as she set her silverware down.

"Sorry, Mom. Caroline is excited, that's all."

Mark opened his mouth to say something about the gift but he saw a storm brewing in Angela's eyes and put in a mouthful of roast beef instead.

Cathy spoke next, calm but emphatic.

"I didn't give you a car. I bought you a house."

Angela choked on her roll.

"You didn't tell me it was a house!" She stared at her mother, blushing. Out of the corner of her eye, she saw Kate looking at Cathy and Mark looking at her. She couldn't see what Papa was doing. She wanted to crawl under the table—no, out the door.

Why, oh, why did we come here? For Caroline—all this was for Caroline. When did mother buy me a house?

"But you said the music CD went with it," Caroline said, undeterred by the silence.

"It does," Cathy said. "That's part of the surprise. There's a music studio in the basement. That's something you don't find every day."

Angela looked nervously at Mark, who was now staring, open-mouthed, at Cathy. "Uh, thank you, Mom. That is—I had no idea—doesn't the CD go with a car? With the trouble I've had with my truck from time to time, I assumed you'd bought a car."

"I didn't know about your truck. I just knew you needed a home, especially after the fire."

Tears welled up in Angela's eyes.

"Grandma, did you say we could see it, somewhere on the other side of Sutton?"

"Sutton?" Angela repeated.

"Yes, it's over on—"

"Hickory Street," Mark said instantly. "Four bedrooms, screened porch, and music studio in the basement? There's only one house like that in Sutton, and it's on Hickory Street."

"Yes. Did you know the former owners?" Cathy asked.

"No, but I've seen it." He looked at Angela. "It's a good house."

Angela shook her hair over her eyes as she wiped her mouth with the napkin. Don't cry. *Not now, not here.* She was grateful when Mark asked his sister about her latest documentary and the dinner conversation turned to something other than her and the house. She tried to listen to all the details of Kate's film, but she still couldn't grasp what her mother had done for her.

"So the Cedar Fire, driven by the Santa Ana winds, burned more than 250,000 acres that year," Kate concluded.

"Sounds like quite a project," Mark said.

Angela wished she hadn't loaded her plate so full.

Would it be rude to leave as soon as we're done eating?

Caroline had questions about the farm and the damage the vandals had done. Papa and Mark talked about the clean-up effort and the help from so many caring neighbors.

"There's no better place to live than Sutton," Papa said.

Angela checked her mother's reaction to that statement, but

Cathy was staring out the window, lost in another place or time.

"Why would anyone want to damage those beautiful trees?" Cathy asked with a certain melancholy in her voice that Angela didn't recognize.

"Buried treasure," Papa said. "They tried to dig under the trees to find it."

"We don't know that," Mark said.

"What treasure?" Caroline asked.

"Our great-grandparents settled this land and buried a treasure on it. It's what makes our trees different." Papa finished his sentence and stood to clear his empty plate. "That meal was delicious. Thank you, Mrs. Shaw."

"I had lots of help from Kate," Mrs. Shaw replied.

"We *think* they buried a treasure." Mark tried to clarify what Papa said. "No one has actually seen it." He picked up his plate and started toward the kitchen door.

"Your dad saw it," Cathy said. She moved her gaze from the window to Mark.

Mark almost dropped his dish. He stared at Cathy and looked to Angela for confirmation, but shock and confusion clouded her features.

"What did you say?" he asked.

"Your dad, Greg—he told me he found it."

Papa set his plate down. Mark did too.

"Do you have a root cellar?" she asked. "He said he put it there until he could figure out what else to do with it. That was right before we graduated." She paused and looked out the window again. "I thought he'd made it up. He told me he'd show it to me, but that never happened." Cathy's voice grew quieter. "To be honest, after he married your mother—and I don't mean any disrespect, I wasn't sure what to believe."

CHAPTER 26

The group moved to the room with the fireplace, and Mark and Kate listened to stories about their parents as Cathy and Papa shared what they remembered. Mrs. Shaw added tidbits of things Donna had told her. Caroline sat next to Angela, and the conversation came full circle to the buried treasure.

Cathy detailed the conversations she had with Greg and what he'd told her about the box he had found. He had been excited, but he hadn't told her what was in it.

"He wanted to *show* me," Cathy said. "I believed him, but when I returned from Maine and he and Janey were married, I assumed he'd made it up. I'm sorry, but you can understand why I doubted him. I never knew my father had told him I was engaged. I wasn't." She stopped talking and looked down at her hands.

"You don't have to be sorry," Kate said. "Papa, did you tell my dad not to look for the treasure because you wanted it to stay buried? Is that why he didn't tell you he found it? If he took it out of the ground, would the trees stop creating miracles?" she asked.

Her question hung in the air, and all eyes turned to Papa.

He rubbed his forehead. "I've seen a lot of miracles in my time. I don't know for sure if that treasure is there or not," he said. "There are good people who believe. They have faith, and miracles happen."

"I certainly didn't expect I'd get to eat Christmas dinner with my daughter and granddaughter this year," Cathy admitted, "and especially not here."

Papa continued, "That's what I mean." He looked at Mark. "You're keeping the farm—and the trees. I'd say a changed heart is a about the sweetest miracle a man can have."

Caroline perked up and she whispered something to her mother. Angela shook her head. "What is it?" Mark asked.

"Is the treasure still there in the root cellar?" Caroline asked.

No one answered at first. The quiet farmhouse settled around them, and they looked into each other's faces.

"There's only one way to find out," Papa said. He stood up and grabbed his coat and Mark's from the rack. "Here."

"I want to come," Kate said.

Mark looked at Angela, longing filled his heart. "Do you want to come with us?"

"Let's go," Papa said. "We won't all fit inside that root cellar, but the walking will feel good."

"Yay," Caroline cheered, and they all bundled up.

The late-afternoon sun filtered through low clouds and the air stirred around them as they walked to Papa's cabin. The cellar was used for the storage of equipment and other odds and ends they didn't use. The ceiling was low, and it couldn't fit more than two of them, three at the most.

"What a funny bunch you are. I'm not climbing in there in my holiday clothes," Mrs. Shaw declared.

Papa suggested Mark and Kate go take a look.

"Do you see anything that looks like a treasure box?" Mark joked.

"It's hard to see anything in here," Kate said. "Maybe we should have brought flashlights."

"Or shovels," Mark added. He lifted a few pruning tools.

They emerged a short time later without finding anything.

"Come with me, Cathy. Let's check it out," Papa said with the excitement of a schoolboy.

Angela stood a few feet from the door of the root cellar. Caroline held her new necklace with one hand and her mother's hand with the other, squirming with excitement.

Mark approached them. "It may not be here. My dad probably

moved it. On fifty acres, it could be buried anywhere." He looked over the damaged trees and beyond. "But thank you for coming. This has been quite a week, treasure or not."

Angela nodded. "I'd say this is our most memorable Christmas yet. What do you think, Caroline?"

"Yep." She nodded.

"I hope I can . . . see you again," he said to Angela.

"I'd like that," she replied. "And I can't get over that my mom knew your dad in high school. Does it bother you at all that they talked about getting married?"

"No, I guess it doesn't. If anything, I understand what Papa means when he says there's more to this life than what we can see."

Papa surfaced and Cathy came out brushing off her coat.

Mark grabbed Angela by her free hand. "Let's go look one more time."

Angela was still holding Caroline's hand. They piled into the eight-foot-by-eight-foot cellar.

"Can we find anything you and Papa didn't?" Angela asked. She squinted to see what was stacked in the corner.

Mark gestured toward Caroline "I thought she'd burst if she didn't have a chance to look around."

Angela couldn't see his features very well in the dusty-dim light, but she liked him all the more for saying that.

"Papa and I will have to come out one day with a shovel and dig out this floor."

"What's this?" Caroline pulled at a box on a makeshift shelf.

"Don't touch—it might topple," Angela warned.

"Just a box of gardening tools," Mark said. He lifted it off the shelf and set it down.

Caroline pointed. "No, this," she said. In the wall behind where the box had been, there appeared to be a cavity covered by some boards.

Mark tugged on one and then pulled harder. The second and third board came down more easily. There at rest in the wall sat a box, smaller than a trunk, almost obscured by the years of dirt covering it. Mark reached for it and coughed in the plume of dust.

"Is that it? Is it?" Caroline asked.

Angela stared in awe.

Mark wiped it off with his arm. The latch contained no lock, and the stiff hinges gave way as he opened it.

All three of them converged over the top of it.

"What's in it?" Caroline asked.

Mark set it down and lifted out the contents as carefully as he could. He held up a leather pouch.

"What's in here? Is this dirt?" He handed it to Angela so Caroline could have a look.

He reached in, felt along the bottom of the box, and pulled out a handful of coins.

"Maybe we better get Papa in here. He could tell us what some of this is."

"I can tell that's a pine cone," Caroline said.

Mark gently picked up one of the several pine cones and handed it to Caroline.

"Please be careful with that," Angela said.

"These are seeds on the bottom," Mark said. "Very old seeds, I think."

Mark's hand formed around another object, different than the others. He held it up to the light coming from the door. A small diamond-studded band.

"That's a ring!" Angela exclaimed.

Caroline went running out of the cellar, shouting, "We found it! It's here! We found it!"

In the adrenaline rush of unearthing the treasure, Mark took Angela's hand and slid the band on her finger.

"Um, what are you doing?" Angela protested.

"Just seeing if it fits," he said playfully.

"Nice try." She laughed, took off the ring, and handed it over to him.

He put it in the box. "You like giving things back, don't you."

"Only things that don't belong to me. Besides, you should have at least kissed me first," she teased.

"You're right. Maybe I should give you something I wouldn't mind if you returned." He leaned across and kissed her, long enough to surprise both of them.

Caroline had come back. The others crowded the entrance and blocked the fading sunlight.

"Come on. Let's bring this to the house," he said.

"Land sakes!" Papa exclaimed when Mark handed him the box. "Been in there all these years, has it?"

"Right where he said he put it," Cathy marveled.

155

"Let's go inside and have a look," Papa said. "We'll put it back later."

The sun dipped below the western ridge of trees as they headed back to the farmhouse. Papa with the box clutched under his arm, Mrs. Shaw, and Kate led the way. Caroline held her grandmother's arm as they followed. Mark slipped his hand into Angela's and they walked side by side not far behind the others. Another Christmas Day had come to a close. Mark felt the wind at his back and looked over his shoulder.

The trees are peaceful tonight.

Mark surveyed the land in the other direction, where the back lot of trees had been wounded.

Maybe now the land can start to heal.

"So did you and Caroline ever have a Christmas miracle?" Mark asked.

"That depends on what you mean by *miracle*," she said. "I have a new job—and apparently I even have a new house."

"And you and your mom?"

"We're getting there," she admitted.

"We discovered the treasure," Mark added. "I mean, after all these years, who knew?"

Angela looked at the trees, and up ahead at Caroline. She took a quick glance at Mark.

"You and I found our faith. If that isn't a treasure, I don't know what is."

"And we found each other." He glanced in her direction and squeezed her hand. "I think that's my miracle."

"Mine too."

ACKNOWLEDGMENTS

When I set out to write this story, I knew I would need help. What I didn't know was how incredible the ladies of ANWA would be. Skilled and supportive, their encouragement enabled me to press on through numerous revisions and see this novel through to completion.

I give heartfelt thanks to Valerie Ipson and Peggy Urry, my allies in the whirlwind. To all my ANWA sisters who have lent a listening ear and offered valuable feedback: Jennifer Williams, Susan Haws, Georgia Fritz, Raejean Roberts, and Anika Arrington. As well as Joyce DiPastena, Nancy Anderson, Carroll Morris and many others who gave much needed advice all along the way.

To my willing and patient beta readers: Kristin Cinelli, Amy Cowan, Heather Hunter, Valerie Ipson, Susan Jensen, Elaine Obeniski, Melanie Passey, Melody Peterson, Cathy Thompson, and Peggy Urry.

To those who helped answer some of my tougher research questions: Spencer Passey, Sofia Richman, Emily Harding, Kimball Cody, Keri Hughes and Meghann Gavin.

To Tristi Pinkston for her masterful editing and Laura J. Miller for her brilliant artistry with the cover. And to E A Smart III for his spot-on illustrations.

To my sister Jorie Raine Fradella for her unfailing support, superior creative instincts and for still answering my calls. To my dad and especially my mom—for being the opposite of Angela's mother in every way—and for listening to all the poems and stories I wrote as a child.

To my son Steven, for all things technical and to my daughters, for their hugs and smiles that carry me through the hardest of days, writing or otherwise.

And to my husband, Steve, for finding me. And not letting go once he did.

ABOUT THE AUTHOR

Tamara Passey was born and raised in Massachusetts around a large family, one that has served as inspiration for most of her writing. She loves creative endeavors and when she isn't writing or re-writing, you can find her baking or cross-stitching or walking—though not all at the same time. She is a marriage and parenting contributor to FamilyShare.com and lives with her husband and three children in Arizona—which she claims might be the reason her stories include a little bit of snow. *The Christmas Tree Keeper* is her debut novel. You can find her online at www.TamaraPassey.com.